NUALA O'MALLEY: A STORY OF IRELAND

H. BEDFORD-JONES

NUALA O'MALLEY

A STORY OF IRELAND

H. BEDFORD-JONES

STEEGER BOOKS • 2019

PUBLISHING HISTORY

"Nuala O'Malley: A Story of Ireland" originally appeared in December 30, 1916–January 20, 1917 issues of *All-Story Weekly* magazine (Vol. 66, No. 2–Vol. 67, No. 1). Copyright 1916–17 by The Frank A. Munsey Company.

"About the Author" originally appeared in November 16, 1929 issue of *Argosy* magazine (Vol. 208, No. 1). Copyright 1929 by The Frank A. Munsey Company. Copyright renewed in 1957 and assigned to Steeger Properties, LLC. All rights reserved.

TABLE OF CONTENTS

NUALA O'MALLEY:
A STORY OF IRELAND

CHAPTER I

THE BLACK WOMAN

THE HORSEMAN reined in as his jaded steed scrambled up the shelving bank, and for a space sat there motionless, for which the horse gave mute thanks. The moon was struggling to heave through fleecy clouds, as it was hard on midnight; in the half obscurity the rider gazed around suspiciously.

There was nothing in sight to cause any man fear. Behind him rippled the Dee, and all around was desolation. Ardee itself lay a good two miles in the rear, burned and laid waste six weeks before, and ten miles to the south lay Drogheda. Indeed, as the horseman gazed about, he caught sight of a faint glare on the horizon that drew a bitter word from his lips.

Dismounting with some difficulty, owing to his cloak and Spanish hat, he examined a long, raking gash in his horse's flank; then flung off hat and cloak and calmly proceeded to bind up his own naked shoulder beneath.

His was a strange figure, indeed, now that he stood revealed. He wore no clothing save breeches and high riding-boots; an enormous sword without a sheath was girt about his waist, and the caked blood on his shoulder and cheek made his fair skin stand out with startling contrast.

About his shoulders fell long hair of ruddy yellow, while his face was young and yet very bitter, tortured by both physical and mental anguish, as it seemed. He bound up the deep slash in his shoulder with a strip of cloth torn from his cloak, felt his wealed cheek tenderly, then flung the cloak about him again and drew down his broad-brimmed hat as he turned to his weary horse.

"Well, my friend," and his voice sounded whimsical for all its rich tone, "you've had a change of masters to-day, eh? I'd like to spare you, but man's life is first, though Heaven knows it's worth little in Ireland this day!" With that he reeled and caught at the saddle for support, put down his head, and sobbed unrestrainedly.

"Oh, my God!" he groaned at length, straightening himself to shake a clenched and blood-splashed fist at the sky. "Where were You this day? God! God! The blood of men on Thine altars—"

"Faith, you must be new come to Ireland, then!"

At the shrill, mocking voice the man whirled about and his huge blade was out like a flash. But only a cackling laugh answered him, as down from the bank above slipped a perfect hag of a creature, and he drew back in alarm. At that instant the moon flooded out; his sudden motion had flung off his wide hat, and he stood staring at the wrinkled creature whose scanty garments and thin-shredded gray locks were pierced by a pair of weird brown eyes.

Then he quivered indeed, and even the poor horse took a step backward, for the old woman had flung up her arms with a shrill cry as she gazed on the yellow-haired young man.

"The O'Neill!" The words seemed to burst from her involuntarily. She craned forward, her hands twisting at her ragged shawl, and a flood of Gaelic poured from her lips as she stared at the awe-struck man.

"Are you, then, the earl, come back from the dead? Ghost of Tyr-owen, why stand you here idle in the gap of Ulster, where once Cuculain fought against the host of Meave? Do you also stand here to fight as he fought—"

"Peace, mad-woman!" exclaimed the young man, stooping after his hat. "Peace, and be off out of my way, for I have far to ride."

The Gaelic words came roughly and brokenly from him, but

the old hag took no heed. Instead, she advanced swiftly and laid her hand on his arm, still gazing into his face with a great wonder on her wrinkled features.

"Who are you?" she whispered. "Tell the Black Woman your name, if you are no ghost! For even as you stand now, once did these eyes see the great earl himself."

"I am from Drogheda," answered the man, something very like fear stamped on his powerful and bitter-touched young face. "My name is Brian Buidh, and I ride to join Owen Ruadh—"

"Liar!" The old woman spat forth the word with a cackle of laughter. "Oh, you cannot fool the Black Woman, Yellow Brian! Listen—Brian your name is, and Yellow Brian your name shall be indeed, since this is your will. Owen Ruadh O'Neill lies at the O'Reilly stead at Lough Oughter, but you shall never ride to war behind him, Brian Buidh! No—the Black Woman tells you, and the Black Woman knows. Instead, you shall ride into the west, and there shall be a storm of men—a storm of men behind you and before you—"

"For the love of Heaven, have done!" cried Yellow Brian, shrinking before her, and yet with anger in his face. "Are you crazed, woman? Drogheda has fallen; O'Neill must join with the royalists, and never shall I ride into the west. Be off, for I have no money."

He turned to mount, but again she stopped him. It seemed to him that there was strange power in that withered hand which rested so lightly on his arm.

"The Black Woman needs no money, Yellow Brian," she cackled merrily. "You shall meet me once again, on a black day for you; and when you meet with Cathbarr of the Ax you shall remember me, Brian Buidh; and when you ride into the west and meet with the Bird Daughter you shall remember me.

"So go, Yellow Brian, upon whose heart is stamped the red hand of the O'Neills! *Beannacht leath!*"

"*Beannacht leath,*" repeated the man thickly.

There was a rustle of bushes, and he was alone, wiping the cold sweat from his face.

"Woman or fiend!" he muttered hoarsely. "How did she know that last? Yes, she was crazed, no doubt. I suppose that I do look like the earl—since he was my grandfather!"

And with a bitter laugh he climbed into the saddle and pushed his horse up the bank. The bushes closed behind him, the night closed over him, but it was long ere the weird words of the old hag who called herself the Black Woman were closed from his mind.

For, after all, Yellow Brian was of right not alone an O'Neill, but The O'Neill.

CHAPTER II

THE BEGINNING OF THE STORM

THE PEOPLE of every nation—that is, the tillers of the soil, the people who form the backbone of their race—are in continual expectancy of a Man and a Day. Theirs is always the, perhaps, dumb hope, but still the hope, that in their future lie these two things, a Man and a Day. Sometimes the Man has come and the Day has failed; sometimes the Day has come and there has been no Man to use it; but now all Ireland had swept up in a wild roar, knowing that the Man and the Day had come together.

And so, in truth, they had. Owen, the Ruadh, or red, O'Neill, had fought a desperate struggle against the royalists. Little by little he had cemented his own people together, his personal qualities and his splendid generalship had overborne all else, and the victory of Benburb had crowned the whole. Then Owen Ruadh was stricken down with sickness, Cromwell landed and stormed Drogheda, and Yellow Brian had fought clear and fled away to the kinsman he had never seen.

Now, standing on the castle ramparts overlooking Lough Oughter, Yellow Brian stared moodily out at the lake. His identity had been revealed to none, and the name of Brian Buidh had little meaning to any in Ireland. Years since he who was The O'Neill, the same whom the English called Earl of Tyr-owen, had fled with his family from the land. His eldest son John had settled at the Spanish court.

John was a spineless man, unworthy son of a great father,

content to idle away his life in ease and quiet. And it was in the court of Spain that Brian O'Neill had been born, with only an old Irishwoman to nurse him and teach him the tongue and tidings of Ireland which his father cared nothing for.

Yellow Brian had written out these things, sending the letter to the sick general who lay within the castle. His terrible news of Drogheda had created consternation, but already O'Neill's forces had been sent to join the royalists against the common foe. All Ireland was distraught by war. Royalist, patriot, and Parliament man fought each against the other, and the only man who could have faced Cromwell lay sick unto death.

The Day was passing, the Man was passing, and shadow lay upon all the land.

A man came up and touched Yellow Brian's arm, with word that Owen Ruadh would see him at once. Brian nodded, following. He was well garbed now, and a steel jack glittered from beneath his dark-red cloak as he strode along. Upon his strong-set face brooded bitterness, but his eyes were young for all their cold blue, and his ruddy hair shone like spun gold in the sunlight; while his firm mouth and chin, his erect figure, and his massive shoulders gained him more than one look of appreciation from the clustered O'Reillys.

He followed the attendant to a large room, whose huge mantel was carven with the red hand and supporting lions of the clan Reilly, and passed over to the bed beside the window. He had requested to see O'Neill alone, and the attendant withdrew silently. Brian approached the bed, and stood looking down at the man who was passing from Ireland.

Sharp and bright were the eyes as ever, but the red beard was grayed and the face was waxen; a spark of color came to it, as Owen Ruadh stretched forth a hand to take that of his visitor.

"Brian O'Neill!" he exclaimed, in a voice singularly like that of Brian himself. "Welcome, kinsman! But why the silence you enjoined in your letter?"

"My name is Yellow Brian," answered the younger man

somberly. "I have none other, general. You know the gist of my story, and here is the rest. I broke with my father, for he would hear nothing of my coming to Ireland. So I cast off his name and left him to his cursed idleness, reaching Drogheda barely in time to take part in the siege. I managed to cut through, as you know, and meant to take service with you—"

He paused, for words did not come easily to him, as with all his race. A low groan broke from the crippled warrior.

"Too late, kinsman, too late! Cromwell is come, and I will never sit a horse again—ah, no protests, lad! How old are you?"

"Twenty-three."

"By my faith, you look thirty! Lad, my heart is sore for you. I am wasted and broken. I have no money, and Cromwell will shatter all before him; I can do naught save give you advice."

"I want naught," broke in Brian quickly, a little glint as of ice in his blue eyes. "Not for that did I cast off my name and come to—"

"Tut, tut, lad!" O'Neill reproved him gently. "I understand, so say no more of that matter. You are Brian Buidh, but to me you are my kinsman, the rightful head of my house. You can do two things, Yellow Brian—either follow my advice, or go down to ruin with all Ireland. Now say, which shall it be?"

Brian gazed at him with thoughtful face. What was the meaning of this dark speech? As he looked into the keen, death-smitten eyes of the man who might have saved Ireland, he smiled a little.

"I see naught but ruin, Owen Ruadh," he replied slowly. "I care little for my life, having no ties left on this earth—"

"Oh, nonsense!" broke in the other impatiently. "You are young, lad—the bitterness will soon pass, trust me. Now see, here is my advice, such advice as I would give no other man alive. I am dying, Yellow Brian. Well, I know that Cromwell will break down all I have built up, and I can see no brightness for my country. But for you I can see much. You are young, powerful, the last of the old race; you look strangely like the old earl, Brian!"

The younger man started. For the first time in many days he remembered that crazed hag he had met by the Dee water the night of Drogheda.

"Now, harken well. I tell you that our house lies in the dust, Brian; there is no hope for it or for any O'Neill. But for Yellow Brian there is hope. You must carve out a holding for yourself, for you are a ruler of men by your face, lad. Go into Galway, and there, where Cromwell's men will have hardest fighting of all, gather a force and make head. I have heard strange tales of a man who has done this very thing—they say he has seized on a castle somewhere near Bertraghboy Bay, in Galway, and— But I am getting weak, Brian lad. Hearken well—Ireland is lost; carve out now for your own hand, for the Red Hand of the old house, lad! And take this for my sake."

Almost whispering the last words, Owen Ruadh took from his finger a signet graven deeply with the Red Hand of Tyrowen. Brian accepted it gravely, kissed the hand that gave it, and with tears choking his throat, left the chamber of the man who was passing from Ireland.

He had been there a brief fifteen minutes, yet it seemed that an age had passed. Both he and the sick man had said much in few words, for they were both men who spared speech and did much. But Brian had received a great wrench.

As he had said, he had cast off his father, for the grandfather's blood ran riot within him, and had kindled to burning rage against the sluggard who had made his name a thing of reproach in all lands. With the overstrong bitterness of youth he had meant to die sword in hand, fighting for Ireland. The few burning words of Owen Ruadh had stripped all this false heroism from him, however, and had sent a flame of sanity into his brain.

Brian returned slowly to the round tower, and stood looking out over the waters, for the castle was built on an island in the lake a mile from shore. It was nearing sunset, and snow was in the air—the first snow, for this was the end of September.

"Ruin—the storm of men!" He repeated unconsciously the

words of the hag who had stopped him by the Dee water. "What shall I do? Which is the part of a man, after all; to fall for Ireland or to hew out new lands and found a new house in the west? By my hilt! That old hag told me truly after all!"

At that thought he stood silent, his eyes troubled. What was this fate which seemed to drive him into the west, instead of leading him to the flame of swords as he had so long hoped and dreamed? Death meant little to him; honor meant much. All his life he had lived in Spain, yet it had been a double life. He had ridden and hunted and learned arms with the young nobles of the court, but he had talked and sorrowed and dreamed with the old Irishwoman who had nursed him.

After all, it is often the dreams of the youth which determine the career of the man, he reflected.

Which path should he take? As he stood there struggling with himself, his hand went unconsciously to his long, powerful jaw; it was a gesture habitual with him when in deep thought—which he seldom was, however. Now the youth in him spoke for death, now the sanity which had flashed into his brain from that of the sick man spoke for the life of deeds and renown which lay in the west.

An incident might turn him either way—and the incident came in the shape of a very tall old man who wore the Irish garb of belted, long-sleeved tunic and woolen hose, with iron-soled shoes. The old man's face was cunning, but his eyes were bright and keen and deep gray; his gray hair hung low to conceal his lopped ears, and there hung about him an indescribable air of shrewdness faced with apparent openness of heart.

Brian glanced at him, remembered that he had heard him called Turlough Wolf, and looked away carelessly, absorbed in his own thought. But the old man halted abruptly with an exclamation:

"*Corp na diaoul!* Where got you that face and that gesture, Drogheda man?"

Brian looked at him, frowning.

"What mean you, Turlough Wolf?"

The other stared, his thin jaw fallen.

"Why—why," he stammered, "I thought it had been The O'Neill come to life again! When I was a boy I have seen the earl hold his hand to his chin—often, often! And—and you look like him, Brian Buidh——"

"Nonsense!" Brian forced a laugh, but as he folded his arms again the glitter of O'Neill's ring on his finger caught the sharp gray eyes.

Turlough Wolf started.

"Listen!" he said, coming forward insinuatingly. "Yellow Brian, no man knows who you are, nor do I ask. But Turlough Wolf knows a man when he sees one, a chieftain among men. I owe no man service; but if you will need a swift brain, a cunning hand, and an eye that can read the hearts of men, I will serve you."

Brian looked down into the shrewd face in wonder, then waved an impatient hand.

"No use, Turlough Wolf. I have no money to pay for service, and to-night I must ride out to seek I know not what—nay, whether I ride west or east or south, I know not!"

He turned abruptly, wishing to close the matter, but the old man laid a restraining hand on his shoulder.

"I seek no money, Yellow Brian. I seek only a master such as yourself; a man who is a master among men, and whom I can set higher still if he will heed my counsels. I am old, you are young; I know all parts of the land by heart, from the Mayo shore to Youghal, and I am skilled at many things. Take my service and you will not regret it."

Brian hesitated. After all, he considered, the thing came close to being uncanny. The Black Woman by Dee water; Owen Ruadh himself, and now this Ulysseslike Turlough Wolf— whither was fate driving him? Was he really to meet such persons as the Bird Daughter and Cathbarr of the Ax, or were they only the figment of a crazed old woman's brain?

So he hesitated, gazing down into those clear gray eyes. And as he looked it seemed to him that he found strange things in them, strange urgings that touched the chords of his soul. After all, adventure lay in the west, and he was young!

"Good!" he said, gravely extending his hand. "To-night we ride to the west, you and I. Come; let us see O'Reilly about horses."

And this was the beginning of the storm of men that came upon the west.

CHAPTER III

THE DARK MASTER

"THERE ARE two things, Yellow Brian, for you to mind. First, you must have men at your back who know you for their master; second, you must stand alone, giving and receiving aid from no man or party in the land."

Brian nodded and stored away the words in his heart, for in their three weeks of wandering he had learned that Turlough Wolf was better aid than many men. It was his doing that, when they had chanced on a party of ravagers beyond Carrick, Yellow Brian had been led into strife with their leader. The upshot of that matter was that there was a dead rover; Yellow Brian had a dozen horsemen behind him and money in his purse, and of the dozen none but feared utterly this silent man who fought like a fiend.

To the dozen had been added others—four Scotch plunderers strayed from Hamilton's horse and half a dozen Breffnians from Ormond's army, who had been driven out of Munster by the rising of the Parliament men there. They were a sadly mixed score, of all races and creeds, but were fighting ruffians to a man, and were bound together by Brian's solemn pledge that he himself would slay any who quarreled. The result was peace.

So now, with a good score of men behind him, Yellow Brian had ridden down into Galway, was past Lough Corrib and Iar Connaught, and was hard upon Connemara.

There was a thin snow upon the hills, and the bleak wind presaged more; but the score of men sang lustily as they rode.

Two days before they had come upon a dozen strayed Royalist plunderers, and had gained great store of food and drink—particularly drink. So all were well content for the time being.

"Turlough," asked Brian suddenly, as they rode side by side, "did you ever hear of one called the Black Woman?"

The Wolf crossed himself and grimaced.

"That I have, Yellow Brian, but dimly. They say she deals in magic and sorcery, and no good comes of meeting with her. But stop—there are horsemen on the road! Scatter the men, and quickly; let us two bide here."

There was cunning in the advice, for the two had come to a bend in the road and the men were a hundred yards behind them. Brian drew rein at sight of a score of men a scant quarter-mile away and riding up the hill toward them. He knew that they must also have been seen, but his men would still be out of sight, so he turned with a quick word:

"Off into the rocks, men! If I raise my sword, come and strike. Off!"

As he spoke he bared that same huge cut-or-thrust brand he had borne from Drogheda and set the point on his boot. Instantly the men scattered on either side the road, where black rocks thrust up from the snow, and within two minutes they and their horses had disappeared.

The riders below came steadily forward in a clump, and Brian saw old Turlough staring with bulging eyes. Then the Wolf half caught at his bridle, as if minded to fly, and his hands were trembling.

"What ails you, man?" smiled Brian. "Are they magicians and sorcerers, then?"

"No, *fareer gair*—worse luck!" blurted out the other. "Look at the little man who rides first, Yellow Brian!"

Brian squinted against the snow-glare, and saw that the leader of the approaching party seemed indeed to be a little man with hunched shoulders and head that glinted steel.

"A hunchback!" he exclaimed. "Well, who is he?"

"The Dark Master—O'Donnell More himself! It is in my mind that this is a black day, Brian Buidh. O'Donnell More is the master of all men at craft, and the match of most men at weapons. Beware of him, master, beware! I had thought that he was still under siege at Bertragh Castle, else I had never taken this road."

"Nonsense!" laughed out Brian joyously, drinking in the clear afternoon air. "So much the more honor if we slay him, Turlough Wolf! Let him match me at weapons, or you at wits, if he can!"

Turlough muttered something and drew back behind Brian's steed with pallid face. Yellow Brian, however, having a sure trust in his own right arm and his hidden men, scanned the approaching O'Donnell curiously, seeking what had inspired such unwonted fear in the old gray Wolf.

He could find nothing ominous in that hunched figure, save its mail-coat and steel helm. Yet the face was peculiar. Over a drooping mustache of black flared forth two intense black eyes. Brian noted this, and the thin, curved nose and prominent chin, and laughed again.

"Who is this Dark Master, Turlough?"

The other shivered slightly. "He is an O'Donnell from the north, come here some ten years since—he seized on Bertragh even as we intend seizing on a stead, and has since done evil things in the land. Now hush, for they say the wind bears him idle talk."

Brian's thin lips curved a trifle scornfully, but he kept silence, watching the approaching men. At fifty yards' distance they halted. Their leader eyed the motionless pair for a moment and then slowly rode on alone, waving back his followers. And Yellow Brian made a strange figure, with his ruddy hair streaming from beneath his steel cap and the bright, naked sword rising up from toe to head beside him.

"Well?" O'Donnell More's voice was deep and harsh, though Brian afterward found that it could be changed to suit its owner's mood. "Who are you thus disputing my passage?"

"I am Brian Buidh," came Brian's curt reply. "As for dispute, that is as you will."

"Yellow Brian?" The black brows shot up in surprise. "A strange name. Whence come you, and seeking what?"

"I seek men, O'Donnell More." Brian swiftly determined that this was a man who might give him aid, a man after his own heart. "Whence I come is my affair. Give me men, and I will repay with gold."

"What need have you of men, Yellow Brian," came the sardonic answer, "when your own lie hidden among the rocks?"

Now indeed Brian started, whereat the other smiled grimly.

"How knew you that?"

"If you recognized me from afar, you had not stayed to meet me unless you had men," stated O'Donnell shrewdly enough.

"True," said Brian, and laughed out. "Well said, O'Donnell. I have a score, and want another score. I will match mine against yours, or make a pact, as you desire."

The Dark Master sat fingering his sword-hilt and considered. With the black brows down and the black eyes fixed on him, Brian suddenly began to like the man less.

"I will give you service," returned O'Donnell at last.

Brian smiled. "Men serve me, not I them."

At this curt answer O'Donnell looked black, then fell into thought, his shoulders hunched up and his head drawn in like the head of a turtle. Brian wished now that he had struck first and talked afterward.

Finally the Dark Master looked up with a slow smile.

"Welcome to you, Brian of the hard eyes and hollow cheeks," he said. *"Slaintahut!"* I will not give you men, but I will give you the loan of men if you will do me one of two favors. Ten miles to the south of here there is an old tower on a cliff, and in the tower dwells a man with certain companions who sets me at naught. On an island out near Golam Head is a castle where a woman rules, who has also set me at naught. Go, reduce either of these twain, and I will lend you twoscore men for three months."

Brian sat his great horse and looked at the Dark Master. He would have sought advice from Turlough Wolf, save that he did not like to turn his back on those burning eyes. After all, the pact was not a bad one.

"These enemies of yours—who are they, and what force have they?"

The Dark Master chuckled, and his head shot out from between his shoulders.

"The man is called Cathbarr of the Ax, and he is a hard man to fight, for he has ten men like himself, axmen all. The woman cannot fight, but she has a swift mind, many men, and her name is Nuala O'Malley, of the O'Malleys of Erris."

"I had sooner fight a man than a woman," returned Brian slowly. "Also, this Cathbarr of the Ax has fewer men. I will do you this favor, O'Donnell Dubh."

He gave no sign of the wonder that had shot into his mind at the name of Cathbarr, except that his blue eyes seemed changed suddenly to cold ice. The Dark Master saw the change, and his smile withered. Brian, watching him, reflected that this malformed freebooter could be venomous-looking at times.

"I have passed my word," O'Donnell the Black made curt answer. "Fetch either of the twain to Bertragh, dead or alive, and you have the loan of twoscore men for three months, free. Is it a pact?"

"It is a pact," answered Brian, and at that the other galloped back to his men.

Brian swung his sword and flung it high into the air; before it had flashed down to nestle in his palm again, his men were scrambling into the road. He sheathed the sword, smiling a little, and turned to Turlough.

"Well? To your mind or not, Wolf?"

"My father saw the Brown Geraldine at Dublin," responded that worthy, scratching the gray beard which had begun to sprout. "They broke his bones with the back of an ax and swung him out in a cage until he died, and after. He made pacts too easily."

"Well?" asked Brian again, but a dull flush crossed his cheeks.

"I gave you my rede," said Turlough sullenly. "I said to stand alone, receiving aid from neither man nor faction. Now there is mischief to be repaired."

"Then my sword shall repair it," said Brian, and ordered the men to swing in after him. "Guide us to this tower of Cathbarr's, for my honor is in my own keeping."

They swung about and headed to the south and the sea.

The hill-paths, which Turlough Wolf seemed to know perfectly, were cruelly hard on the horses; none were as yet trodden down, for the snow was fresh, and all the west coast lay desolate. The plague had stricken Galway and Mayo heavily that year, smiting the mountains with death. Some few parties of Roundhead horse had come through, because they feared God and Ireton more than the plague, and some Royalists had fled up from the south for much the same reason.

In any case, Yellow Brian found all the land desolate, and liked it. The more wasted the land, he reflected, the more chance for that sword of his to find swinging-room. As he had ridden, news had come from the east—news of the Wexford killing and the curse that was come upon the land. Owen Ruadh O'Neill was not yet dead, but Brian knew that he had prophesied truly. Ireland's day was gloaming fast.

Despite the dismal tone of Turlough Wolf, Brian told himself that he had done a good day's work. O'Donnell Dubh would keep his word beyond any question. As for the man he was to slay, the only part of it which troubled Brian was the prediction of the Black Woman at the Dee water. She had known him, and had prophesied O'Neill's death, and had spoken of the west and this Cathbarr of the Ax. After all, however, she might have shot a chance shaft which had gone true. Brian had no faith in magic.

All that afternoon he rode on, Turlough Wolf ahead of him,

the men behind. They feared and hated the old Wolf as much
as they feared and loved Brian.

Progress was slow, owing to the bad paths, the snow, and
sundry changes of direction, so that when night fell they had
covered but eight miles of the ten. Turlough suggested that they
push on and finish their business at a stroke, but Brian curtly
refused. So the men made camp in lee of a cliff and proceeded
to feast away the last of their provisions and wine, in confidence
that on the morrow they would have more, or else would need
none.

Brian and Turlough built a fire apart, and after their repast
Brian broke silence with a request for information about Cath-
barr. It was his first speech since the parting with the Dark
Master.

"I never heard of him," responded Turlough. "No doubt he
is some outlaw who has become a thorn in the Dark Master's
flesh. With the woman it is different."

"Tell me of her," said Brian, gazing into the fire.

"She is an O'Malley, and, like all the clan, makes much of
ships and seamen and little of horses and riders. When the Dark
Master came, ten years ago, he slew her father and mother by
treachery, and would have slain her but that her men carried her
off. She was a child then. Now she is a woman, very bitter against
O'Donnell Dubh, and is allied with the Parliament so that her
ships may have the run of the seas, it is said. O'Donnell takes
sides with no faction, but caters to all. He lays nets and snares,
and men fall into them, and he laughs."

"Why is Nuala O'Malley called the Bird Daughter?" asked
Brian quietly.

At this question old Turlough rose on his elbow, and in his
wide, gray eyes was set mingled fear and wonder.

"M'anam an diaoul!" he spat out. "Who are you to know this
thing?"

"Answer my question," returned Brian, hiding his own
surprise.

"Seven years ago, master, I was at Sligo Bay with O'Dowda when Hamilton cut us to pieces. Nuala O'Malley had brought us some powder—she was but a slip of a girl then. In the evening I was down at the ship when I saw her come from below, a hooded pigeon in her hands. She whispered in the bird's ear, set off the hood, and the bird flew into the night. I named her Bird Daughter, but no other man knew the name."

"Then a woman did," chuckled Brian dryly. "It was but a carrier pigeon, Turlough; I have seen them used in Spain. Now listen to me."

With that he told him of the Black Woman and his weird meeting at Dee water. Old Turlough listened in no little amazement, for he was full of superstitious fancies, but Brian said nothing of his own name. The uncanny prophecies, however, which now seemed on the road to fulfilment were enough to give any man pause.

When he had finished, a very subdued Turlough Wolf stated that the Black Woman was an old hag who wandered all over the land, that some called her crazy and others thought her inspired, and that his own belief was that she was a banshee, no less.

At this Brian saw the thing in a more rational light. The old woman knew of this nook in the west, and, attracted to him by his resemblance to the long-dead earl, she had endeavored to steer him thither. After all, it was quite simple.

Of course, old Turlough swore that he had never breathed his name of Bird Daughter to a living soul, and that it was but a name he had used in his own mind for the slim girl who had fetched powder from the south. Brian chuckled, guessing that Turlough was not the only one who had seen carrier pigeons used, and who had ascribed the thing to higher powers.

The incident served the purpose of establishing a firmer intimacy between Brian and the old man, however, and convinced Turlough that his master was destined to fly high. Nor through all the storm of men that befell after did Turlough again breathe reproof as he had dared that day.

"I begin to see that your advice was good, Turlough Wolf," said Brian the next morning, as he rode shivering from camp. "As to making my men know me for their master, that troubles me little; but I think it will be a hard matter to avoid making pacts, and to stand alone."

"Lean on your sword," grunted old Turlough. "To my notion, such friendship as that huge blade of yours can give is better than good. Order men ahead."

Brian nodded and sent two of the men ahead as scouts, with the Wolf himself. For the better part of an hour they made slow headway among the rocks, and then emerged suddenly on the slope leading down to the cliffs and sea. Turlough pointed to the left.

"There lies the tower, if I mistake not."

Drawing rein, Brian saw at once why he had been sent on this errand. Cathbarr's tower was an old ruin at the end of a long and narrow headland—indeed, at high tide most of the headland would be covered, for it was low and yet beyond shot of the cliffs. Except from the water, it was almost impregnable; cannon might have reached it from shore, but two axmen could have held the narrow way against an army.

Brian laughed softly and ordered the men to remain where they were.

"What are you going to do, master?" queried old Turlough anxiously.

"I am going to lean on my sword, as you advised me," chuckled Brian, and rode on alone.

CHAPTER IV

BRIAN LEANS ON HIS SWORD

A S HE had foreseen, Brian was allowed to ride across the narrow neck of land where his men would have had to battle for progress. It was from no mere bravado that he had gone forward alone to the tower, but because men were worth saving, and he believed that his own sword was a match for any ax. If this ruffian Cathbarr was a freebooting outlaw, he would be willing enough to stake his ten men on his prowess, and Yellow Brian was very anxious to have those ten axmen behind him.

At the top of the tower men watched and steel glistened, and as Brian rode up to the low gateway, it was flung open and a man strode out. This man hardly came up to Brian's conception of an outlaw, except as to stature.

He was a good six feet four, reflected Brian as he drew rein and waited, and was built in proportion—or, rather, out of proportion. His shoulders and chest seemed tremendous, and a long mail-shirt reached to his knees; his hair was short-clipped and brown, and beneath his curly brown beard Brian made out a massive face, wide-set brown eyes, and an air not so much ruffianly as of cheerful good-humor.

Brian had no need to ask his name, however, for in one hand he carried a weapon such as had seldom seen the light since powder had come to Ireland. It was an ax, some five feet from haft to helve; double-bladed, each blade eight inches long, curved back slightly, and two inches thick by twice as much wide. The edges, which came down sharply from the thickness, were not overkeen, and were not meant to be so. When the thing struck, that was the end of what stood before it.

"*Cead mile failte!*" cried Cathbarr of the Ax in a deep, rumbling voice, his white teeth flashing through his beard in a smile. "A hundred thousand welcomes to you, swordsman! Are you come to capture my lordly castle?"

"No; your men," laughed Brian, liking this huge, merry giant on the instant. "I am come from O'Donnell Dubh to reduce you and fetch you to him."

The smile froze on the giant's face.

"I am sorry for that, yellow one! I like your face and your thews, and to find that you serve the black traitor of Bertragh is an ill thing."

"I serve no man," answered Brian easily. "I need men. If I conquer you, O'Donnell lends me twoscore men for three months; also, by conquering you I win your men to me, which makes fifty. With my seventy men, I shall fall to work."

"By my faith, a ready reckoner!" and Cathbarr grinned again. "Get down and fight."

Brian swung out of the saddle and led his horse to one side. They were not so badly matched, he reflected. Cathbarr's head was bared, while he had steel cap and jack; but for some reason he felt hesitant at thought of killing this merry giant.

"Not so bad," he said, baring his five-foot blade and holding it up against the huge ax. "Not so bad, eh?"

Cathbarr burst into a laugh.

"It will grieve me to crush your skull, dear man," he rumbled. "What a pair we would make, matched against that Dark Master! But enough. Ready?"

Brian nodded slightly, and the long ax flashed up.

Now, Brian O'Neill had served a stiff apprenticeship at weapons, and had faced many men whose eyes boded him death, but here, for the first time in all his life, he felt the self-confidence stricken out of him.

As Cathbarr heaved up his ax, he became a different man. All the good cheer fled out of his face; his curly brown beard seemed to stand out about his head like snakes, and the massiveness of his body was reflected in the battle-fury of his face. He needed no blows to rouse him into madness; but with the ax swinging like a reed about him, he came rushing at Brian, a giant come to earth from of old time. His men on the tower set up a wild yell of encouragement.

Brian leaped swiftly aside and, thinking to end the fight at a blow, brought down his sword against the descending ax-haft. Sparks flew—the haft was bound with iron; Brian only saved himself from falling by a miracle.

Then began a strange battle of feet against brawn, for Cathbarr rushed and rushed again, but ever Brian slipped away from the falling ax, nor was he able to strike back. The play of that ax was a marvel to behold; it was shield and weapon in one, and it seemed no heavier than a thing of wood as it whirled. Twice Brian got in his point against the mail-coat without effect, and twice the ax brushed his shoulder, so that he gave over thrusting. He knew that he was fighting for his life indeed.

An instant later he discovered that fact anew as a glancing touch of the ax drove off his steel cap and sent him staggering back a dozen paces, reeling and clutching at the air. To his amazement Cathbarr did not follow him, but stood waiting for him to recover; he had not looked for such courtesy on the west coast.

He sprang back into his defense, desperate now. Again the ax whirled, seeming a part of the giant himself, and Brian knew that he was lost if he waited for it. So, instead of waiting, he leaped under the blow, dropped his sword, and drove up his fist into the bearded chin, now flecked with foam.

It was a cruel blow. Cathbarr grunted, his head rocked back, and he swayed on his feet. Before he could recover, Brian had set his thigh against him, caught his arm, and sent him whirling to the ground, ax and all. Then he picked up his sword and stood leaning on it, panting.

Cathbarr sat up and gazed around blankly, until his gaze fell on the waiting figure. Brian looked at him, smiling slightly, and the eyes of the two men met and clinched. As if he had been a child caught doing wrong, the giant grinned and wiped the foam from his beard.

"Was that fair fighting, yellow man?" he asked.

"No," laughed Brian. "It was unfair, Cathbarr; but I think my fists can best your ax yet."

Slowly the giant got to his feet. To Brian's surprise he left his ax where it lay and came forward with extended hand.

"Had you claimed that blow as fair," he rumbled, "I would have slain you. Now I love you, yellow man. Let us make a pact together. What is your name?"

They struck hands, and Brian felt a great thrill of admiration for this man whose terrible strength enclosed the simple heart of a child. But he shook his head.

"I make no pacts, Cathbarr. My name is Brian Buidh. I made pact with the Dark Master, and now I am sorry for it; yet it must be held to, for I see no way out of it. But wait—I have a cunning man whose wit may help us here."

He turned and flung up his sword in the air. His men rode down to the narrow causeway, while from the tower came shouts warning Cathbarr against treachery. But the giant only grinned again, and Brian shouted to Turlough Wolf to come on alone.

Old Turlough obeyed in no little wonder. When he came up Brian told him what had chanced—that out of enmity had arisen friendship.

"But," he concluded, trouble in his heart, "you must find me a way out, Turlough. I have passed my word to O'Donness to reduce Cathbarr; to do that I must slay him, or he me. I see little honor either way."

"Few men find honor in their dealings with the Dark Master," grumbled Turlough, looking from Cathbarr to Brian. "Yet, if you want a way out, it is an easy matter. Cathbarr of the Ax, give service to my master. Thus, Brian Buidh, you shall reduce

Cathbarr; yet the Dark Master said naught of giving up this man to him."

"Good!" cried Brian, eagerness in his blue eyes, and swung on the giant. "Will you give me your service, friend, and follow me? There shall be a storm of men—" He paused abruptly as the words fell from his lips, but he had said enough.

"I give you service, Yellow Brian," rumbled Cathbarr, taking his hand again, and his strong, white teeth flashed through his beard. "I will follow you, and my men, and there shall be firm friendship between us. Is it good?"

"It is good!" exclaimed Brian, his heart singing. But Turlough laughed harshly.

"So you have again broken my rede, Brian Buidh, for this man knows you not as his master, but names you his friend. I bade you take, not give."

"It was your own advice," retorted Brian, laughing.

"Aye, since you asked it, I found the way out. But you have not conquered him."

"He conquered me by not telling a lie," said Cathbarr simply. "I serve him."

Turlough eyed them keenly, heard how the fight had gone, and then suddenly comprehended what manner of man this huge, bearded fellow was. His face cleared, and without a word he clasped Cathbarr's hand, and asked Brian for orders.

"How far from here is Bertragh Castle?" questioned Brian.

"It overlooks Bertraghboy Bay," answered the giant. "Bide here till noon, while my men bring in their horses from the hills, and with the night we can arrive there."

To this Brian assented, well pleased that Cathbarr had horses. Turlough went back to bring up his men, and Brian entered the tower that served Cathbarr for castle. It was a small place, but strong; the ten men who took his hand and gave him service were cut after the pattern of their master—huge fellows all, O'Flahertys from the mountains who had followed Cathbarr down to loot the coast, with no ill success.

It was a strange tale that he heard, while he and his men ate and drank with their new comrades. For some months Cathbarr had maintained himself here, raiding O'Donnell's lands chiefly and making his ax feared through all the coast. In fact, the giant had attempted his own errand—to set himself up in power; but he had gone about it like a child.

The Dark Master had come against him with a hundred men, and after losing a score and more at the causeway, had tried to starve him out. At that Cathbarr had calmly stolen away by boat, raided O'Donnell's choicest farms overnight, and was back with his plunder before the Dark Master guessed his absence. After this O'Donnell had kept watch and ward upon his lands, with better results; Cathbarr occupied himself with raiding against the scattered parties of plunderers in the hills, and had won some booty.

Brian discovered many things during the hour or two he waited for the horses to be fetched in. Chief of these was that he had set himself a difficult nut to crack. The Dark Master held a strong castle, with rich farms around it, and could summon at need some three hundred men to his standard. In short, Brian found that O'Donnell held the very position he himself wanted to hold—and was like to keep it.

"Of course," he thought soberly, reflecting on his future course, "if I come off clear to-night I can ride with my seventy men to a better place. And yet—I don't know! What better place than this? It will be no long time before hoofs are in the land, for Royalist and Roundhead and Ulsterman will be storming through the hills; Galway will be the last to give in to Cromwell, of a certainty. When the hurricane falls, I want a roof to shelter me—and whom could I turn out better than this O'Donnell?"

Cathbarr's tower was too small to serve him as a fortalice, for it was barely large enough to shelter the eleven axmen. Suddenly an idea flashed across Brian's mind. Why not a union with this O'Malley woman against the Dark Master?

Upon the thought, he rose and went out to the ice-rimmed

shore below the tower, where he paced up and down, considering
the matter. After all, it would do no harm, and there were great
possibilities in it. He returned to the tower at sound of shouts
and clattering hoofs, and took Turlough aside.

"Turlough Wolf, in your advice you spoke against making
pacts with men, but you said nothing of women. It is my purpose
to send you to this O'Malley castle, to propose a pact with Nuala
O'Malley against the Dark Master. You can tell her that I have a
hundred horsemen behind me—for I will have them. Will you
do this, bearing her word back to me?"

Turlough plucked moodily at his ragged beard.

"I see no harm in such a pact, master," he replied thoughtfully. "As to reaching the Bird Daughter, that is another matter.
I think that I can do it, however. When shall I start, and where
shall I find you again?"

Brian reflected a moment.

"Start now, Turlough. Cathbarr and I will have no need of
advice this night, for we shall either fight our way clear, or else
the Dark Master will keep to his word. When you return, you
will find me here; if I am not here, I will leave a man here to
give you word of me."

"I am to say that you have a hundred horsemen behind you?"
Turlough's sharp eyes swept to Brian's half-questioningly.

"Say a hundred and a half," laughed out Brian, "and trust your
silver tongue for the rest, old Wolf! Never fear, I will have the
men. But mind this, Turlough. I will make no other pact with
her than this, against the Dark Master. It may be that when I
have driven him forth I may fly after other game."

"Men have sought to drive the Dark Master forth," quoth
Turlough, "and their heads have rotted above his gate. Take
heed lest there be an empty spike there this night, Yellow Brian!"

But Brian only laughed shortly, and bade the old man
affectionate farewell, for he knew that Turlough loved him.
And when Turlough had ridden somberly away, Brian felt a
strange sense of desertion, of loss, that was no whit inspired

by Turlough's gloomy last words. He shook it off, however, at gripping hands again with Cathbarr. The axmen had gathered most of their loot and buried what was of value, for Brian had determined to return here from Bertragh and make use of the tower until he had heard from Turlough's errand.

So now, at the head of thirty men, he rode across the narrow causeway with Cathbarr of the Ax at his side for friend and guide. The giant did not yet quite comprehend exactly what plan had flashed across the brain of old Turlough, so as they rode Brian made the thing clearer to him. When the simple and straightforward Cathbarr grasped the matter, he smote his horse's neck with a bellow of laughter.

"Ho! So you bring me before the Dark Master ax in hand, reduced to *your* service instead of his, my men added to yours— oh, it is a jest, brother, a jest! I think that O'Donnell will slay us both on the spot!"

"Not if your axmen are true," retorted Brian.

Cathbarr laughed again. "They fear me and they love me, brother," he cried, gazing back at the file of horsemen. "Your own men fear you and love you also. Therefore we are men alike."

Brian began to love the man for his utter simplicity, save where there was killing in hand. Cathbarr seemed in reality to have the heart of a child, impulsive and passionate to an extreme, and there was always a certain rugged power in his bearing which bespoke him a true Flaherty of the mountains. His men were like himself in this respect, and after they had fraternized with Brian's men they began to feel the same unbounded surety in Yellow Brian as Cathbarr expressed. Their axes were the usual splay-bladed affairs that their grandfathers had used under Red Hugh at the Yellow Ford, nor indeed in all his life had Brian ever seen another ax like to that of Cathbarr's.

They rode through the afternoon while a light snow fell and a keen east wind cut down from the peaks of the Twelve Pins, until the shaggy horses slithered along with tails tucked tight beneath them. But there was good cheer in the company, for the news had spread of how Yellow Brian would have seventy men behind him that night. When the darkness began to fall, Bertragh Castle came in sight far below—a gray crag jutting up from the plain, scarped and embattled, the sea behind it and the watch-fires of men twinkling from its keep. All about lay farms and steads, and the lowing of byred cattle rose on the evening air when the snow ceased.

"Be careful not to drink or eat in that hall," warned Cathbarr blackly. "Ill comes of it to all who accept hospitality there."

Brian nodded and rode on in silence, for there were parties of horsemen and pikemen down below and the blare of horns shrilled up. Evidently the riders on the hills had been seen from afar.

As they reached the lower ground Brian was aware of a band of men riding to meet them, and halted. Through the dusk came a score of armed horsemen, and their leader inquired their business, shouting from a safe distance. Brian returned the shout.

"I am Yellow Brian, and I seek O'Donnell Dubh according to a pact made with him yesterday. I have reduced Cathbarr of the Ax, and am come in peace."

"You are expected," called the other, riding up with his men. "The Dark Master is waiting for you."

And Brian rode on to Bertragh, not without some forebodings.

CHAPTER V

YELLOW BRIAN RIDES SOUTH

OUTSIDE THE castle gates, where cressets flared over the snow, an old seneschal appeared and ordered Brian to leave his men outside. To this the men made some objection, but Brian laughed softly.

"Bide where you are," he said. "You shall not be slain unless I am slain inside."

The O'Donnells watched him and Cathbarr with no little wonder, and the two men made a fine pair as they marched across the creaking drawbridge. Though Cathbarr topped Brian by half a head, there was no doubt as to which was the nobler man; the giant gazed around him with amazed eyes, but Brian held his head high and strode in with a smile flickering on his lips. But his blue eyes were very sharp that night.

He saw the crowded men in the courtyard, many of them armed with muskets, their matches burning, and noted also that the Dark Master possessed some half-dozen bastards— immense, nine-foot pieces mounted on huge carriages, with their eight-pound balls piled beside them. In those days it was no small thing to own such cannon in the west of Ireland, and Brian eyed them approvingly as he passed through the court- yard. He was beginning to count them as his own.

Cathbarr had told him that the Dark Master had brought many O'Donnells down from the north to settle the farms and lands beyond the castle, but Brian saw that these were not all.

The garrison was a riffraff of all the armies that had wasted Ireland, and they were fighting men fit for their work.

Brian entered the hall, with Cathbarr muttering oaths a pace behind him. The hall was high, lit with cressets, and beside a huge fireplace sat the Dark Master in a carved chair of black wood, an old harper sitting opposite. Behind Brian and Cathbarr flocked in men until the hall was well filled.

Brian found the penetrating eyes fixed on him as he advanced, but in them was no surprise or fear, and O'Donnell calmly stroked his drooping mustache as he watched. Cathbarr still followed behind, bearing that great ax of his, and Brian stopped a few paces from the hearth as the Dark Master spoke.

"Welcome to Bertragh, Yellow Brian. I had not looked for you so soon."

"No." Brian's voice rang out richly in the stillness. "But I am here, O'Donnell Dubh, to claim my two-score men. I have reduced Cathbarr of the Ax."

For the first time the hunched O'Donnell seemed to notice Cathbarr. His black eyes flickered curiously to the giant, then he smiled sourly.

"If he is reduced, why does he not kneel, Brian of the hard eyes?"

"Kneel," ordered Brian.

Cathbarr flushed and his beard began to stand out, but he obeyed. There was no great love in his face as he knelt, holding to his ax, and gazed at O'Donnell.

"Throw your ax into the fire," said the Dark Master, his voice smooth as silk.

"Do not," exclaimed Brian, and his eyes grew bitterly cold as they clinched with those of the Dark Master. Over the latter's pallid face crept a slow red fire, and his head drew back between his shoulders. Men held their breaths.

"O'Donnell," went on Brian slowly, "I have fulfilled my pact. I have reduced Cathbarr of the Ax—but he serves me and not you. Since I have conquered him as you bade, I call on you to carry out the pact and lend me two-score men for three months, scat-free."

If Brian had wanted any testimony as to O'Donnell's iron hand, he had it. His words, with all they implied, would have drawn a howl of rage from the retainers of any other chief in the land, but the men behind and around him only grew more silent.

As for the Dark Master, the red hue died slowly from his face, though his head remained drawn in, and still his eyes held those of Brian. When he spoke, it was as if he were musing aloud.

"So, Brian of the hard eyes, you have some courage, eh? *Duar na Criosd!* Little did I ever think that a man would come to me and borrow my own men that he might make war upon me! Is this your thought, Yellow Brian?"

"You have sharp ears, Dark Master," said Brian dryly, and a chuckle passed through the crowd. "In time I might take this castle, it is true. Just now I have other things in mind, however, and I shall not fall upon you until there has passed gage of battle between us."

"Thanks for so much," smiled the other slowly, though the red crept up to his cheek-bones faintly. Brian seemed perfectly at his ease, as indeed he was. "And what if I fell upon you first?"

"I am liker to offer battle than accept it, O'Donnell."

"Now, that is a good answer," said the Dark Master, while a whisper floated around the hall. "I would be glad to have you at my back, Yellow Brian, for men who ride behind me are like to win much."

Brian laughed a little.

"Some day I may be at your back, O'Donnell Dubh, and in that day I may win all that you have, from life to goods."

To his blank amazement, O'Donnell only threw out his head and chuckled; but it was an evil chuckle, and there was venom gleaming in his black eyes.

"I think that it were best for me to slay you here, Brian of the hard eyes, to slay you and this Cathbarr of the Ax. It seems to my mind that it is anything but good to turn you loose upon the land, for I hear a storm of hoofs in the air, and dead men are riding on the wind, and there is a whisper—"

He paused, drew his cloak about him, and gazed down at his foot. That pause was more dreadful than speech, for the crowded men moved not a finger, so that Brian all but thought that he and the Dark Master were alone. Then his face blanched a trifle. For, whether it were some uncanny play of mind or very truth, it seemed to him that from the wide fireplace there did indeed come a faint ring of hoofs and clash of steel; the long cressets over them suddenly flickered smokingly, though no draft crossed their faces.

Then indeed Brian knew that his fate hung upon the Dark Master's thoughts, and he drew himself up a little straighter, and his blue eyes glinted colder than any ice as his hand closed upon his sword-hilt. But at the slight motion O'Donnell looked up keenly.

"You have ridden hard, Brian. Pause and sup with me—"

"I did not come to eat or drink," said Brian sternly. "Also, I am weary of this talking. Now fulfil your pact, Dark Master, or be shamed before all your men."

"Are you for Royalist or Parliament?" asked O'Donnell, as if he had not heard.

"I am for Brian Buidh."

"Take two-score men and begone," and the other rose. To his surprise, Brian found that, despite the hunched back, O'Donnell was as tall as himself. The black eyes flamed out at him for an instant. "I will keep my honor, though I regret it later, Yellow Brian. Go, with your men. When next we meet your head shall grin over my gates."

"Thanks for so much," retorted Brian mockingly, though he drew a swift breath of relief. "My head serves me too well to render it easily. *Slan leat*, O'Donnell!"

"*Slan leat*," repeated the Dark Master and turned his back, gazing down at the fire.

Brian turned and strode down the hall, Cathbarr at his heels.

When they reached the courtyard he found men saddling in haste, and an officer saluted him gravely.

"Two-score men are at your orders, Yellow Brian."

"Let them follow me," said Brian curtly. "And who quarrels with my men, dies."

To that there was no dispute. The drawbridge clanked down once more, Brian and Cathbarr mounted and rode out to where the thirty waited grimly, and after them came the forty men from the garrison. Cathbarr, who trusted the Dark Master little, set his ten axmen in the van, followed with Brian, and the sixty followed them into the night.

"I think we came out of that well, brother," said the giant softly. "Where do we ride?"

"To your tower, for the night. After that, in search of more men."

"Toward Galway or Slyne Head?"

"Wherever there are men."

After that they rode on in silence, while the men behind fraternized freely. All were of the same stamp, and indeed the two-score already were as willing to serve Brian as O'Donnell, since they had witnessed that scene in the castle hall.

Brian wondered dully what the outcome of all this was to be. The strain of facing O'Donnell and bearding him in his own den had been no light one, but he knew that Cathbarr had spoken truth in saying that they were well out of it. The Dark Master, he thought, was a man well worth fighting. To take his castle was not like turning out a chieftain of some ancient family, with his clan about him for miles around; O'Donnell had seized upon the place himself, his men were reavers and outlaws, and the castle was a strong one.

Then there was the O'Malley alliance. Brian had it in mind to beset the Dark Master by sea and land at once, for all the O'Malley clan had been seamen and rovers from time immemorial, while he himself preferred men and horses at his back. In calmer mood now, he reflected that Turlough might not return for a week, and there was food and fodder for seventy men and horses to be obtained.

If he rode toward Galway he would have to plunder the patriots, which went against the grain. But in lower Galway and Clare things were different. That winter no army held to winter quarters save that of Cromwell, and between Limerick and Galway there was a wild rout of men out of half a dozen armies, the plague had swept off all but the seafaring folk, and men held only what their swords could guard.

So Brian determined that he would ride toward the south.

He realized well that his men must be drawn together by fighting, that they must learn a perfect confidence in him, and that they must earn their sustenance for the time being. Cathbarr already knew of old Turlough's mission, and of course approved, since in his eyes Brian could do no wrong. What was more, reflected Brian, he could not make this alliance empty-handed. He must get men and spare horses, stores and powder, and some muskets or pistols if possible, for few of his men carried more than sword or perhaps a sorry pistolet or ancient bombardule out of date a generation since.

"A storm of men!" he muttered as he gazed at the stars. "A storm of men! Did that Black Woman speak truly, I wonder? And what dark magic was that which passed to-night?"

But no answer came to his questions save that the cold stars chilled him to the bone. Since they had no better place to seek, they returned to Cathbarr's tower, but it was long past midnight when they reached it, and the men were nodding in their saddles. As barely a dozen could crowd into the place, the rest were forced to camp outside in the snow, but roaring fires and some little food put them in good humor and it was no hardship to any of them.

"It has been a strange two days for us twain," said Brian as he and Cathbarr divided a scorched bannock one of the Scots had hastily turned out over the coals.

"Yes," smiled the giant into his beard, his deep-throated bull's voice rumbling through their tiny room. "But it is in my mind that there are stranger days ahead of us, Brian Buidh. A witch-woman once told me that I would meet my death from water and fire together, brother, in a cause not mine own."

"You are not bound to my service," replied Brian.

"But I am bound to you, for I like you," answered Cathbarr, and his hand crushed down on Brian's. That night they slept together beneath the same blanket, and though after that they spoke few words of love or friendship, the two men drew ever closer each to the other in all things.

It had indeed been a strange two days for him, thought Brian as he roused up the camp late the next morning and set out sentries in the hills. He had met the Dark Master on the first, and on the second he had met Cathbarr, then had forced the Dark Master into lending him men against his will. Now, after a scant three days beyond Lough Corrib, he had twined his fate with that of other men, had set his heart upon winning Bertragh Castle, and had won both a stout friend and a stout enemy.

For he counted O'Donnell as a foe, in which he was not far wrong.

However, there was no time to be wasted, for fodder was exceeding scanty, and Brian himself had no heart for idleness. As he had resolved on his course during that return ride the night before, he gathered his men together and briefly ordered them to be ready to ride at noon, and to Cathbarr alone he outlined his plan. Then he picked two of the axmen who knew the country roundabout, and ten from among those O'Donnell had loaned him, and took them aside and told them of Turlough Wolf, who would come before long.

"You will bide here," he concluded, "and bid him wait for me. I shall return this side of ten days. And mind you, if there is feud or treachery among you so that one man's blood is let, then I will exact a tenfold vengeance from both men."

The twelve, who were sturdy ruffians and well able to hold the place against any sudden attack by the Dark Master, looked into the ice-blue eyes for an instant, and straightway vowed that there would be neither treachery nor quarreling among them. And Brian guessed shrewdly that he had inspired some little fear in their hearts.

So that at high noon they rode away to the east, threescore strong, with Brian and Cathbarr and the remaining eight axmen in the van. Brian did not spare either man or horse that day, for there was little food left them; when midnight came they had slipped past Galway and were ready to ride south, though they all went to rest supperless.

With the morning Brian found that two of the men had slipped off and were busy plundering a hill-farm a mile away, where an old woman lived alone. He promptly had them brought before him, and bade them take up their weapons.

"I am no executioner," he said as he bared his huge sword. "I am a teacher of lessons, and my lessons must be learned."

When they rode away from that place, leaving the two men buried under cairns, Brian was well assured that there would be no more ravaging by his men, though they died of hunger.

However, it proved that there was no great chance of this, for Brian drove such a storm past Slieve Aughty as had not been heard of in generations. Of all that chanced in those seven days ere he set his face to the north again, not much has survived, for there were greater storms to come afterward, and more talked-of fighting. But certain things were done which had a sequel.

By the fifth day Brian had swept past Gort toward Lough Graney, and turned west by Crusheen, which he passed through with a hundred horsemen at his heels. Two days before he had struck upon fifty Ulstermen who were working north from Munster, and what were left of them after the meeting took service with him. From them he learned that O'Neill was dying or dead, and that the Royalists and Confederacy men were paralyzed through the south.

They had left Crusheen ten miles behind them on the fifth

day, when Cathbarr laid his hand on Brian's knee and pointed to the left, where a hill rose against the sky.

"Look there, *boucal*—when the birds fly from the *ceanabhan*, seek for snakes!"

Brian drew rein. Gazing at the long slopes of moor-grass that rose across the hill, he saw a sudden flight of blackbirds from over the crest; they flew toward him, then swerved swiftly and darted to the right. Brian called up two of his men who knew the country, and asked them what lay over the hill.

"The Ennis road to Mal Bay," they replied, and he sent them ahead to scout.

Before he reached the hill-crest they were back with word that an "army" was on the road, and Brian pushed forward with Cathbarr to see for himself. Slipping from their horses, they gained the hilltop and looked over on the winding road beyond. Neither of them spoke, but Brian's eyes glinted suddenly, for he beheld a train of four wagons convoyed by some two hundred troopers. He touched Cathbarr and they returned.

"A party of Ormond's Scottish troopers," he said quietly when they had rejoined the men. "Cathbarr, take thirty men and work around them. When you strike, I will lead over the hill and flank them."

The giant nodded, picked his men, and rode away. Brian led his seventy closer to the rise of ground, and as they waited they could hear the creaking of wagons and the snap of whips. It was a Royalist convoy, and since there was no love between the Scots and the Irish of any party, Brian's men were hungry for the fight.

They got their fill that day.

A rippling shout, a scattering of shots, and Brian spurred forward. The road wound a hundred yards below, and Cathbarr had already fallen on the vanguard. The Scots were riding forward to whelm him when Brian's men drove down with a wild yell and smote the length of their flank.

Brian hewed his way to the side of Cathbarr, and then the sword and ax flashed side by side. The captain in command of the troopers pistoled Cathbarr's horse, but the huge ax met his steel cap and Cathbarr was mounted again. Meanwhile, Brian was engaged with a cornet who had great skill at fencing, and his huge Spanish blade touched the young officer lightly until the Scot pulled forth a pistol, and at that Brian smote with the edge.

The muskets and pistols of the troopers worked sad havoc among Brian's men at first, but there was no chance to reload, and when the officers had gone down the Scots lost heart. They would have trusted to no Gaelic oaths, for men got no quarter in the west, but when Brian shouted at them in English they listened to him right willingly. A score broke away and galloped breakneck for the south again, and perhaps fifty had gone down; the rest gathered about the wagons stared at Brian and Cathbarr in superstitious awe as the two lowered bloody ax and sword and offered terms.

"I offer service to you," said Brian. "I am Brian Buidh, and if you will ride with me you shall find war. Those who wish may return to Ennis."

Now, at the most Brian had some seventy-five men left, and those clustered at the wagons were over a hundred and a score, with muskets. But their officers were down, they had received no pay for a year and more, and they were for the most part Macdonalds of the Isles, who loved freebooting better than army work. So out of them all only ten men chose to ride to Ennis again, and Cathbarr shook his head as they departed.

"It seems to me that ill shall come of this," he said, and wiped his ax clean.

Brian laughed shortly and dismounted. He found that the wagons contained powder, stores, and muskets; so after placing the wounded in them, he rode north to Corrofin that day with close to two hundred men at his back. Staying that night at Corrofin, he hanged ten of the Scots for plundering, rested his horses for two days, and set his face homeward with the surety that his men knew him for master.

The storm of men was gathering fast.

CHAPTER VI

BRIAN TAKES CAPTIVES

"*F*AILTE ABHAILE! Welcome, Yellow Brian!"

"So you won back before me, eh?" Brian swung down from his horse and gripped hands with old Turlough Wolf. "Get the men camped, Cathbarr, then join us."

Turlough's cunning eyes rested on the wagons and weary horsemen, and he nodded approvingly as Brian told him of what had chanced.

"Said I not that you were a master of men?" he chuckled quietly, as he turned to follow into Cathbarr's tower. "But it is easier to master men than women, Brian. I bear you a bitter rede from the Bird Daughter, master."

"Hard words fare ill on empty stomachs," quoth Brian. "Keep it till I have eaten."

When Cathbarr had joined them and they had dined well on Royalist stores and wine, Turlough made report on his mission. It seemed that he had met with a party of the O'Malleys at the head of Kilkieran Bay at the close of his first day's ride, and after hearing his errand they had taken him in their ship out to Gorumna Isle, where stood the hold of Nuala, the Bird Daughter. And somewhat to his own amazement, Turlough had found that by this same name she was known along the whole coast.

He reported that it was a strong place, for the castle had been built by her father; that she had two large ships and five small ones, and that both ships and castle were defended by all manner of "shot"—meaning cannon. She had just returned from Kinsale,

where she had been aiding Blake hold Prince Rupert's fleet in
the bay. Now Rupert had slipped away, and after plundering a
French ship with wines, she had come home again.

"She seems a woman of heart," smiled Brian. "What of her
looks?"

"I did not see her." Turlough shook his head. "She ordered
my message written out, so she has some clerkly learning. She
took an hour to ponder it, master, then set me ashore with this
message.

"'Tell Yellow Brian,' she ordered, 'that I claim tribute from
Golam Head to Slyne. I will make no pact with him until he
pay me tribute; and if I find him on my land I will set him in
chains above my water-gate.'"

Brian felt no little dismay at this, for he had counted strongly
on alliance with this Bird Daughter.

However, Turlough proceeded to set forth the reasons for
such a message, as he had conceived them within his shrewd
mind. First, it seemed that the pestilence had visited Gorumna in
the absence of its mistress, and that the Dark Master had caught
a score of the O'Malleys who had been wrecked in Bertraghboy
Bay, promptly hanging them all. Between the plague and the
hanging Nuala had a bare fourscore men left within the castle,
and she counted Brian's offer as a ruse on the part of O'Donnell,
for she was strongly afraid of treachery.

"There is more pride than power in that message," commented
Cathbarr easily. "The Dark Master has stripped away all her
lands along the coast, and save for Kilkieran Bay she has little
left. Let us fall on her, brother, and take what *is* left."

Brian laughed at this naive counsel, looking at Turlough. But
the old Wolf said nothing, brooding over the fire, and Brian
reflected within himself.

He had come into a merciless feud, that he knew well. If
he was to enter upon it he must banish all pity from his heart,
which was no easy thing for him; but Turlough related things he
had heard which speedily changed his mind. There were tales of

O'Donnell's ridings through the land, of men slaughtered and women carried off to people his castle; of treachery, and worse.

It was also whispered that the Dark Master had made alliance with certain pirates from the north coast.

However, Brian knew that he must reach some decision regarding his own men, and that speedily. The three talked long that night, setting aside the question of the O'Malley alliance for the time being. Brian had some two hundred men to house and horses to feed; he had good store of provision and powder, but Cathbarr's little tower was utterly useless to house the tenth of them all, while the stores would have to be sheltered. Then O'Donnell might fling his men on them at any moment, which would mean disaster in their present position.

Cathbarr suggested an attack on Bertragh castle, but Turlough dissented.

"When we strike, we must strike to win," he said shrewdly. "The Dark Master has more men than we, and the sea is at his back, and they say he is a warlock to boot."

The giant stared and crossed himself at talk of warlocks, but Brian laughed out.

"I have a plan," he said, fingering his sword. "O'Donnell watches all the hill-paths like a hawk, even now in winter. Those wagons are of no great use to us, and we can store the goods here in the tower for the present. Get it done to-night, Cathbarr, and get the accouterments from two of those largest Scots for yourself and me."

Turlough Wolf chuckled suddenly, and Brian knew that the old man had pierced to something of his plan. But not all.

"Turlough," he went on as the scheme came to him more clearly, "at dawn ride out with a hundred men to that hill-road where first we met the Dark Master. Hide the men in the hills, and be ready to ride hard when the time comes. Cathbarr, before the dawn breaks have the wagons start out with twenty of the Scots troopers as escort. Bid as many more as can lie down in the wagons and cover up close with their muskets. Send a man or two with them to guide to that hill-road of which I spoke. We will ride after and catch them up shortly after sunrise."

"Good!" roared out the giant, whose brains lay all in his ax. "And the Dark Master will swoop down to the feast, eh?"

"He will not," returned Brian dryly. "He will send two or threescore men upon us, and it is my purpose to take as many of these prisoner as may be."

Cathbarr stared, and Turlough's gray eyes squinted up at Brian.

"How is this, master?" he asked inquiringly. "It is too good a trap to waste on prisoners—"

"My plan is my plan," said Brian briefly. "I am not making war on O'Donnell, but I intend to pay tribute to the Bird Daughter, and that right soon. While we are gone have a score of men remain here and build huts on the cliffs, Cathbarr."

Turlough fell to staring into the fire, divining the plan at length, and Cathbarr went out to fulfil his orders. Brian knew well that there was danger in the scheme, but he determined to deal with one thing at a time, and thoroughly. Just at present he was intent on forming an alliance with Nuala O'Malley, for ships and cannon were needful before he could nip the Dark Master in his hold. It was going to cost the lives of men, and he made up his mind not to pause for that. If he was to live and make head it must be by the strong hand alone—the Red Hand of Tyr-owen; and he looked down at the ring of Owen Ruadh and took it for a symbol, as his ancestors had taken it.

Before they went to rest Turlough pointed out that if the hills were watched he and his hundred would be noted, so Brian bade him hit back toward Lough Corrib and then to come straight down upon the main road. It might be that he could overcome the Dark Master's men of himself, and if not, he would hold them until Turlough came up.

With this plan arranged, then, the four wagons set forth under the cold stars, with thirty Scots lying hidden and twenty riding before and behind. With the first gleam of dawn Turlough and his hundred cantered off to the northeast, and an hour later Brian and Cathbarr put on the buff coats and steel jacks of the troopers, with the wide morions; took a pair of loaded pistols, and galloped after the slow-moving wagons. Brian wore his Spanish blade, but Cathbarr had sent his ax ahead with the troopers.

They caught up with the wagons when the latter were entering upon the road proper out of the hill-track they had followed. The first snows had vanished for the most part, leaving bleak, gaunt hills and rugged crags that twisted with soft fog. The sun struck the fog away, however, and as Brian rode on he gazed up at the purple mountains on his right, and down at the purple bog to his left, and caught the gleam of the Bertraghboy water out beyond. He laughed as he drank in the keen air of morning.

"Best get your edge ready, Cathbarr of the Ax!"

Cathbarr grunted, and slung the heavy hammer-ax at his saddlebow. One of the guides, who were from the Dark Master's twoscore men, pointed to a twisted peak on their right, whence an almost invisible spiral of gray smoke wound up.

"The signal, Yellow Brian," he grinned, cheerfully giving away his secrets. In fact, all those twoscore men rather hoped that their old master would be crushed by Brian, for so long as there was booty in sight they cared not whom they served.

Half an hour later Brian saw ahead of him that same bend of road where first he and Turlough had met O'Donnell Dubh. But there was no sign of Turlough, and he cantered ahead to see if the O'Donnell men were below. As he did so a bullet sang past his ear, and he whirled to see half a dozen of his men go down beneath a storm of lead from the hillsides; at the same instant some three-score men came scrambling down from among the rocks—those same rocks where he had first laid ambush for the Dark Master.

And riders were coming up on the road below!

He was caught very neatly, and caught by more men than he had looked for. The remainder of the twenty gathered behind him and Cathbarr, and the thirty rose among the wagons and for a moment stopped the assault with their musketry; but before the smoke had cleared away two-score horsemen came thundering up the road from behind the curve, and struck.

"Albanach! Albanach!"

The wild yells shrilled up, and the Scots troopers knew that they were fighting without quarter in sight, for the "Albanach," as they were termed in Gaelic, gave and got little mercy in Ireland. The saddles of the fallen were filled from the men in the wagons, and leaving the musketeers to hold off the unmounted men, Brian plunged into the swirl of fighting horsemen and joined Cathbarr.

The odds were heavy, but the big claymores of the Scots were heavier still. Side by side, Brian and Cathbarr plunged through the ranks, sword biting and ax smiting, until they stood almost alone among the O'Donnells, for their men had been borne back. Then the giant bellowed and his ax crushed down a man stabbing at Brian's horse; Brian pistoled one who struck at Cathbarr's back, and pressing their horses head to tail they faced the circle of men, while behind them roared the battle.

For a moment the O'Donnells held off, recognizing the pair, then one of them spurred forward with a howl of delight.

"*Dhar mo lamh,* Yellow Brian—your head to our gates!"

Brian thrust unexpectedly, and the man went over his horse's tail as the ring closed in. So far Cathbarr had forgotten his pistols, but now he used them, and took a bullet-crease across his neck in return; then the ax and sword heaved up together, and the ring surged back. A skean went home in Cathbarr's horse, however, and the giant plunged down, but with that Brian spurred and went at the O'Donnells with the point of his blade. This sort of fighting was new to them, and when Brian had spitted three of them he heard Cathbarr's ax crunch down once more.

They were still cut off from the wagons, but there came a wild drumming of hoofs, and wilder yells from the men on the hillside. Like a thunder-burst, Turlough and his hundred broke on the battle. The O'Donnells were swallowed up, stamped flat; the unmounted men fled among the rocks, Turlough's men after them, and a dozen horsemen went streaming down the road.

It was hard to make the maddened Scots take prisoners, but Brian did it, and when Turlough's men came back he found that they had in all thirty captives. Some forty of the attackers had fallen and the rest had fled.

Since all his captives expected no less than a quick death, Brian ordered ten of them bound on spare horses, of which there were plenty. He himself had lost twenty-three of his Scots, and the remaining score of captives cheerfully took service under him. Then, picking out one of them, he gave the man a horse and told him to ride home.

"Tell your master, O'Donnell Dubh," he said, "that his men made this attack on me, and therefore there is war between us."

The man grinned and departed at a gallop, and word passed through the men that the Dark Master had found his match at last. As to this, however, they were fated to change their opinion later.

"Now," said Brian to old Turlough, as between them they bound up a slash in Cathbarr's thigh, "do you put the wounded in the wagons and begone home again. Set out sentries against an attack from O'Donnell, and scatter a score of men out along the roads to watch for other parties. You might pick up another score of recruits, Turlough Wolf."

Turlough shook his head and tugged at his beard.

"Best take me with you, master, instead of this overgrown ox. You may need brains in dealing with the Bird Daughter, and he has no more brains than strew his ax-edge. Also he is wounded."

Brian pondered this, while Cathbarr furtively shook a fist at Turlough. There was wisdom in the advice, but on the other hand Brian did not like to leave his precious two hundred men in care of Cathbarr. If the Dark Master attacked suddenly, as he was like to do, brains would be more needed than brawn.

On the other hand, he counted on Cathbarr's open face removing the evident suspicion that the smooth-tongued Turlough had raised in Gorumna Isle. It had been a mistake, he saw plainly, to send such an emissary on his mission. Picturing this woman who led her own ships to war, he limned her in his mind as a large-boned, flat-breasted, wide-hipped creature—and with good reason. He had seen women fighting at Drogheda and he had seen them in other places as he rode to the rest, for in those days many a woman took her slain lord's *skean fada* and drew blood for Ireland before she was cut down. And when women rode to battle there was no mercy asked or given, from Royalist or Confederate or Parliament man.

Nuala O'Malley was a woman of blood, said Brian to himself, and he would give her blood for her help.

So he curtly refused Turlough's advice, saw that the ten bridles of his bound and mounted captives were lined together, and beckoned to Cathbarr. Before they rode off, however, they doffed their Scot accouterments and took back their own garments, after which Cathbarr led the way over the hills to Kilkieran Bay, and Turlough took command of the force in sullen ill-humor.

The morning was still young, for the attack had taken place a short two hours after sunrise and had soon been quelled. Beyond a slashed thigh and a red-creased neck, Cathbarr of the Ax was unhurt, and Brian had received no scratch. If the ten captives wondered why they were bound and their comrades freed, they said nothing of it.

Even after seeing what he had of the merciless war in Ireland, Brian had much ado in making up his mind to hold to the plan he had formed on the previous evening. These ten ruffians were scoundrels enough, to judge by looks, and yet they were men; and he had been raised in no such school of war as this, where surrender meant slaughter without pity. However, he determined to do what he could for them, and he would have held to this determination had it not been for what chanced when they rode down to the little fishing village where Turlough had met the O'Malley men.

They arrived just as the evening was darkling, after a hard day's ride.

As they came within sight of the place, which lay at the head of Kilkieran water, Brian made out that a small galley was pulled up on shore, and there were a number of men about the huts. Upon the approach of the two chiefs with their file of captives there was an instant scurry of figures; women ran to the huts, and a dozen or more roughly clad men appeared with pikes and muskets. Brian held up his hand in sign of peace and rode slowly onward, Cathbarr at his side, to within a dozen paces of the huts.

"Who are you?" cried out one of the musketeers. "Be off!"

"Bark less, dog," said Brian, scorn in his eye. "We seek Nuala O'Malley. Take us out to Gorumna Isle in your boat."

"What seek ye with the Bird Daughter?" queried the other suspiciously.

"Her business, not yours."

The seamen gazed at them doubtfully, then a number of other men came from the huts, well-armed. One of these set up a cry, pointing at the captives, and a burst of yells answered him from the rest. Next instant Brian and Cathbarr had their weapons out and were facing an excited crowd of men.

"Be silent, dogs!" bellowed Cathbarr, and his voice quelled the uproar. "What means this attack? Would you have the Bird Daughter strip you with whips, fools?"

The spokesman stood out, his dark face quivering with fury as he pointed.

"That is as it may be, axman, but first those bound men shall die. One is the man who slew my brother, nailing him to his own door till he died; another is he who burned Lame Art's wife and child last Whit-Sunday—"

"There is he who lopped my husband's hands and nose! Slay him!" shrieked out a hag as she burst forward. Brian held out his sword and she drew back, but instantly others had taken up the cry.

"And the devil who hung Blind Ulick!"

"There is he who—"

In that brief moment Brian heard things too horrible for speech. The ten bound men had grouped together, some pale as death, others laughing defiantly. But as the crowd surged forward Brian held up his sword, and they paused to listen; he knew now that there was no more pity in his heart for these black ruffians of O'Donnell's.

"Let the Bird Daughter render judgment upon them," he shouted. "Friends, take us to the Bird Daughter and let her do as she will, for I bear these men to her alone."

At that the crowd fell silent, but their leader gave a rapid order, and half a dozen men ran down to the strand. Another order, and the maddened villagers gave back as the seamen closed about Brian and Cathbarr and their captives.

"Come," said the leader roughly. "You shall go to Gorumna Isle with us, strange men, but I do not think that you shall ever come back again."

"Nor do I," grinned Cathbarr in the ear of Brian, as they left their horses to the fishermen, unbound the prisoners from their steeds, and made their way down to the galley. Brian looked at his friend, and they both smiled grimly.

CHAPTER VII

THE BIRD DAUGHTER

"NOW, *THERE* is a castle worth the taking, Yellow Brian!" said Cathbarr.

Brian nodded, his eyes shining in the starlight. After a pull of a long seven miles down the bay, the galley had rounded into the northern end of Gorumna Isle, guided by a high beacon set among the stars. As they drew nearer Brian made out that this beacon was set on the tower of a high pile of masonry black against the sky, lit here and there by cressets, and it was plain that the Bird Daughter kept good watch since they had more than once been hailed in passing the islands.

Once turned into the harbor, Brian found suddenly that they were among ships, many of them small galleys, but two of good size which bore riding-lights. Again they responded to hails, and without warning a few torches blazed out ahead of them. Then it was seen that the castle was built with its lower part close on the water, and its upper part rising on the crag. In reality, as he found later, it was two castles in one, as of necessity it had to be. Were the opposite isles held by an enemy, and hostile ships in the little harbor, the higher towers running up the crag could dominate all, and the lower castle could be abandoned without danger.

Even in the starlight Brian's trained soldier's eye made out something of this. Then the leader of the seamen came and stood beside them, for during the two-hours' trip he had talked somewhat with Cathbarr and had come to look with more respect on

Brian himself. That was only natural, for seamen ever like those men who talk least.

"Strangers," he said with rough courtesy, "a word in your ear. If you would gain speech with the Lady Nuala, deal not with her as with me. Send in your names and your business, and you may perchance get to see her in the morning, or a week hence, as she may choose."

"Thanks," answered Brian. "But my will is not like to hang upon hers."

The seaman shrugged his shoulders, the oars were put in, and they floated up to where the torches flared. Here there was a landing-place of hewn stone, with a gate lying open beyond it, and armed men waiting. One of these, from his bunch of huge keys and air of authority, Brian knew for the seneschal.

"M'anam go'n Dhia!" he growled, peering down into the boat as it ground on the stone, "what fish have you there?"

"Two salmon and ten herring, Muiertach," laughed one of the men. Brian and his friend stepped out while the ten prisoners were prodded after them, and Brian found the seneschal looking him over with some wonder, hands on hips.

"Well! A giant with a devil's ax, and Cuculain, the Royal Hound, come to life again! Who are you, yellow man, and who is this axman, and who are these ten bound men?"

Brian was minded to answer curtly enough, but he looked at the seneschal and remembered the seaman's kindly warning. Under his eye the laugh withered suddenly on the seneschal's lips.

"These ten men belong to me, Muiertach. Go, tell the Bird Daughter that Brian Buidh and Cathbarr of the Ax have come to her, bringing tribute as she demanded."

Now it was that Cathbarr, who had asked no questions all that day, perceived for the first time the reason of their fighting and hard riding, and what the manner of that tribute was. He broke into a great bellow of laughter so that the rough-clad seamen stared at him in wonder, but at a word from Brian he quieted instantly.

"In the morning the message shall be delivered, Brian Buidh," returned burly Muiertach with a glimmer of respect in his voice. "And now render up your weapons, so that we may treat you as guests—"

"So you sea-rovers are afraid of two men, lest they capture your hold?"

Brian's biting words brought a deep flush to Muiertach's face.

"No weapons do we render," he went on, his voice cold as his eyes. "We come as guests, seneschal, and our business is not with you. Take these ten men to your dungeons, take us to guest chambers and give us to eat, and see that we have speech with the Bird Daughter before to-morrow's sun is high."

At this Muiertach growled something into his beard, but turned with a gesture of assent. His men closed around the captives, while Brian and Cathbarr followed him into the castle, the giant still chuckling to himself with great rumbles of laughter.

"Let strict watch be kept over these two," said Muiertach in English to one of the torchmen who accompanied them, thinking he would not be understood.

"You may yet get a touch of the whip for that order," said Brian in the same tongue.

Stricken with amazement, Muiertach turned and stared at him, jaw dropping, while Cathbarr glanced from one to the other in perplexity. Brian smiled.

"Lead on, and talk less."

With tenfold respect, the seneschal obeyed. Now Brian saw that this castle was indeed a stronghold, and might easily be defended by fewer men than it had. The inner walls of the lower castle were well lined with falcons and falconets, while on the towers above peered out heavier cannon, which he took for culverins from their length of nose. Crossing the courtyard, they entered the building itself, and Muiertach led them through upward-winding corridors, studded with cressets and with here and there a recessed *prie-dieu* in the wall.

From the snatches of talk behind the doors they passed, Brian guessed that this lower castle was occupied by the garrison. In this he was right, for with torchmen before and behind them they emerged into the cold night air again and climbed upward, coming to a gate in the wall of the upper castle. This stood open, but it clanged shut behind them, and after crossing a steep courtyard they entered a second and broader corridor.

Muiertach led them up a long flight of stairs, then another, and finally flung open a heavy door. It was evident that they were lodged in one of the towers.

"Rest sound and fear not to eat our food," said the seneschal. *"Beannacht leath!"*

"Blessing on you," responded Brian and Cathbarr together, and entered.

For a wonder, Brian found that the chamber was lighted with candles, which Cathbarr examined with no little awe. Also, it contained a very good bed, on which the giant looked with suspicion. The hard stone walls were hung with tattered tapestries, and before they had settled well into their chairs two men entered with food and wine of the best.

"Not so bad," smiled Brian as they ate. "How come your wounds, brother?"

"Those scratches? Bah!" And the giant gurgled down half a quart of Canary at a stretch. "You are not going to sleep on that bed of cloths?"

"That I am," laughed Brian, "and soon, for I am overweary with riding. Try it, Cathbarr, and you will be glad of it."

"Not I! Since there is no bracken here the floor is good enough for me. Eh, but this sea-woman will have a thought in her mind over your message, brother!"

Brian chuckled, but he was too weary with that day's work to talk or think, and when the remnants of their meal had been removed and their door shut, he gratefully sought the first bed he had known for weeks. After some laughing persuasion he prevailed on the suspicious Cathbarr to blow out the candles, and upon that he fell asleep.

When he wakened it was broad daylight, and Cathbarr was still snoring with his ax looped about his wrist as usual. Brian, feeling like a new man, went to the open casement and looked out.

He found himself gazing through a three-foot stone wall, and as he was doubtless in one of the towers, this argued that the lower walls were twelve feet thick or more. The lower castle was hid from him, but his view was toward the upper bay and included the harbor. The two larger ships, which were small carracks, but large for the west coast in that day, bore six guns on a side, and Brian saw that they were being scrubbed and made shipshape. The Bird Daughter must be a woman of some scrupulousness, he reflected. Beyond the brown sails of two fishing-boats, and low, storm-boding clouds over the farther hills, there was nothing more in sight.

As Cathbarr still wore his long mail-shirt, Brian kicked him awake, and after his first bellowing yawn their door opened and men brought in jars of water. When the giant's wounds had been dressed, under protest, and they had broken their fast, the seneschal appeared.

"Chieftains," he said respectfully, "the Lady Nuala has received your message and will have speech with you this afternoon. Until then she wishes that you keep your chamber, since she knows not your mind in this visit."

"That is but fair," assented Brian.

Cathbarr grumbled, but there was no help for it, since they were virtually prisoners. The day passed slowly, and toward noon storm drew down on the harbor and snow eddied in their casement. With that, they fell to polishing their weapons; Brian procured a razor and a much-needed shave, and Cathbarr furbished up his huge ax until it glowed like silver.

Finally Muiertach appeared. Brian slung the great sword

across his back, and they followed the seneschal down to the courtyard. Here they were joined by the captive O'Donnells and the seamen who had brought them to the castle, and Muiertach led them to the great hall.

The father of this O'Malley woman must have been a man of parts, thought Brian as he gazed around. The hall was scantily filled with, perhaps, three-score men ranged along the walls, and at the farther end was a low dais where a huge log fire roared high. The beams were hung with a few pennons and ship-ensigns, and on the dais were placed a half-dozen chairs. Behind one of these stood two women, and in the chair, calmly facing the hall, sat the Bird Daughter.

Brian caught his breath sharply, and his blue eyes flickered flame as he saw her. Never in his life had his gaze met such a woman—not in all the land of Spain or elsewhere in Ireland.

At this time Nuala O'Malley was twenty years old, and ten of those years had been passed either on shipboard or here in Gorumna Isle. As one chronicler describes her, "She was not tall, but neither was she small of stature, and when she stood on a ship's deck there was no tossing could cause her to stumble. Her hair was not blue, but neither was it black, and her eyes were very deep and bright, violet in color, and set wide in her head. Her nose was neither small nor large, her cheeks were ever red with the wind off the sea, her mouth was finely curved, but tight-set withal, and she had more chin than women are wont to have. She was very lissom in body, but her head never drooped."

And that is a most excellent description of the Bird Daughter, in fewer words than most men might use to-day.

But of all this Brian noted at the moment only that before him sat a girl-woman whose calm poise and confident power struck out at him like a vibrant presence. Like himself, she wore a cloak of dark red, but no steel jack glittered beneath it; there was a torque of ancient gold about her neck, and her hair was caught up and hidden beneath a small cap of red.

Brian thought of the woman he had painted in his mind, then

laughed softly. She caught the laugh on his face, and comprehended it, and was pleased; then as she watched him very calmly,
it seemed to Brian that her sheer beauty was a thing of decep-
tion. It must be, for she was surely a woman of blood. He had
known enough of beautiful women, who played the parts of
men, to know that on the far side of their beauty was neither
mercy nor love nor compassion, that their lovers were many
steps to ambition, and that they were venomous. So his smile
died away, and his blue eyes glittered cold and dark, and this the
Bird Daughter saw also.

Now, there was no man on the dais save Muiertach, who
mounted the two steps with his keys jangling. As Brian would
have gone after him, two pikemen stepped forward to intervene.
Brian looked into their eyes and they drew back again. He and
Cathbarr mounted to the dais, and he bowed a low, courtly,
Spanish bow, of which the Bird Daughter took no note. Instead
he heard her voice, very low and penetrating, and she was speaking to the two pikemen.

"Go out into the courtyard," she said, "and give each other
five lashes. This is because you dared insult a guest, and because
you drew back after insulting him. Go!"

The two pikemen, rather pale under their beards, handed over
their pikes to comrades and strode out of the hall. She turned
to Brian, speaking still in Gaelic:

"Welcome, Brian Buidh. You have come to bring me tribute?"

"Yes, Lady Nuala, and the tribute is these ten men of the
Dark Master's."

She looked at Cathbarr; her eyes swept over his ax. Then she
looked again at Brian, and spoke to Muiertach in English.

"Truly, I have seldom seen such a man as this—"

A swift look of warning flashed over the seneschal's face, and
Brian laughed.

"Lady," he said in the same tongue, "he is Cathbarr of the Ax,
and he will be a good man to stand with us against the Dark
Master."

She betrayed no surprise, except that a little tinge of red crept to her temples.

"I did not know you spoke English, Brian Buidh. Still, it was not to Cathbarr that I referred."

At that it was Brian's turn to redden, and mentally he cursed himself. There was no evil in this woman's heart, he saw at once. For an instant he was confused and taken aback. Then she smiled, slowly rose, and tendered him her hand. Going to one knee, he put her fingers to his lips.

"Now sit, Yellow Brian," she said, "and let us talk. First, these captives of yours. Do you in truth bring them as a tribute? How do I know they are O'Donnell's men?"

"Ask these seamen of yours," laughed Brian, seating himself beside her. Cathbarr remained standing and leaning on his ax, looking like some giant of the old times.

She took him at his word, and when she had heard from the seamen certain tales of what cruelties the ten prisoners had done, her violet eyes suddenly turned black and an angry pallor drove across her face.

"That is enough," she interrupted curtly. "Take them out and hang them."

The men were led away, and Brian saw that her hands were tightly clenched, but whether in fury or in fear of herself he could not tell. Then she turned to him, looking straightly into his face, and on the instant Brian knew that if this girl-woman bade him go to his death, he would go, laughing.

"Tell me of yourself, Brian Buidh. Of what family are you? By the ring on your finger you are an O'Neill; yet I have heard nothing of such a man as yourself leading that sept. When your messenger came to me, I read cunning in his face, and took it for a trap set by the Dark Master; but now that I have seen you and Cathbarr of the Ax, I will take fealty from you if you wish to serve me."

Brian smiled a little.

"Serve you I would, lady, but not in fealty. I take fealty and do not give it. My name is indeed Brian Buidh, and as for that ring, it was a gift from Owen Ruadh."

"Owen Ruadh died two days since," she said softly, watching his face. "I had word of it this morning."   .

At that he started, and Cathbarr's eyes widened in fear of magic. Owen Ruadh had lain on the other side of Ireland, and three months would have been fast for such news to travel. But Brian nodded sadly.

"Carrier pigeons, eh?" he said in English and paused. He knew not why, but his loneliness seemed stricken into his heart on a sudden; he who neither explained nor asked for explanation from any man, felt impelled to open his life to this girl-woman. He crushed down the impulse, yet not entirely.

"Perhaps, Lady Nuala, there shall be greater confidence between us in time, and so I truly desire. But know this much—I am better born than any man in Ireland—aye, than Clanrickard himself; and I am here in the west to seek a new name and a new power. It is in my mind to take O'Donnell's castle from him, lady. I have some two hundred men, of whom the Dark Master himself *lent* me twoscore, and in alliance with your ships we could reduce him."

"How is this, Brian? You say he lent you twoscore men?"

He laughed and explained the fashion of that loan; and when he had finished a great laugh ran down the hall, and the Bird Daughter herself was chuckling. Then he waited for her answer, and it was not long in coming.

"There is some reason in your plan, Brian Buidh, but more reason against it. The castle that O'Donnell holds was formerly my father's. If you held it, there would be no peace between us, unless you gave fealty to me, which I see plainly you will not do. I claim that castle, and shall always claim it."

"Then it seems that I am held in a cleft stick," smiled Brian easily, "since I will give fealty to none save the king, or Parliament. You are allied with the Roundheads, I understand?"

She nodded, watching him gravely.

"Yes. Cromwell is master of the country, and I am not minded to butt my head against a wall, Brian Buidh. If I am to hold to the little that is left me, I shall need all my strength."

"And that is not much, lady. Your coasts are plague-smitten, your men reduced, and Cromwell has not yet won all the country. Galway will be the last to fall, indeed. But as to Bertragh Castle, why should you not sell your rights in it to me?"

At his first words a helpless anger flashed into her face, succeeded by a still more helpless pride.

"No, I will not sell what I have been unable to conquer back, Brian Buidh. If there were any way out of this difficulty with honor, I would take it; for I tell you frankly that I would make alliance with you if I could."

Brian gazed at her, reading her heart, and fighting vainly against the impulse that rose within him. Twice he tried to speak and could not, while she watched the conflict in his face and wondered. He wished vainly that he had Turlough's cunning brain to aid him now.

"Lady," he said at last, biting his lips, "I will do this. I will give you fealty for the holding of Bertragh Castle, keeping it ever at your service, but for this alone. When we have taken it, it may be that I shall render it back after I have won a better for myself; yet, because I would sit at your side and have equal honor with you, and because we have need of each other, I will give you the service that I would grant to no man alive. Is it good?"

For an instant he thought that she was about to break forth in eager assent, then she sank back in her chair, while breathless silence filled the hall. She gazed down at the floor, her face flushing deeply, and finally looked up again, sadly.

"I do not desire pity or compassion, Brian Buidh," she said simply, and her eyes held tears of helpless anger.

Then Brian saw that she had pierced his mind, for which he was both sorry and glad. He knew well there were other castles to be had for the taking, and there was nothing to prevent his riding on past Slyne Head and winning them—except for his meeting with this girl-woman. Therefore he lied, and if she knew it, she gave no sign.

"You mistake me, lady," he said earnestly, his blue eyes softening darkly.

"I propose this only as a stepping-stone to my own ambition. Soon there will be a sweep of war through the coasts, and I would have a roof over my head. Is it good?"

She rose and held out her hands to him.

"It is good, Brian Buidh. Give me fealty-oath, for Bertragh Castle alone."

And he gave it, and his words were drowned in a roar of cheers that stormed down the hall, for the O'Malleys had heard all that passed.

An hour later Cathbarr of the Ax was despatched in a swift galley to bear the tidings to Turlough, and bid him make ready for a swift and sharp campaign.

Through the remainder of that afternoon and evening Brian sat beside the Bird Daughter, and he found his tongue loosened most astonishingly, for him. He told her some part of his story, though not his name, while in turn he learned of her life, and of how her father and mother had been slain by O'Donnell through blackest treachery.

The more he saw of her, the more clearly he read her heart and the more he gave her deeper fealty than had passed his lips in the oath of service. As for her, she had met Blake and others of the Roundhead captains on her cruises, deadly earnest men all; but in the earnestness of Brian she found somewhat more besides, though she said nothing of it then. It was arranged between them that in three days they would meet before Bertragh Castle, by sea and land, and the Dark Master would be speedily wiped out.

With the morning Brian set forth to join his men in the largest sailing galley, for a wild gale was sweeping down from Iar Connaught. But the O'Malleys were skilled seamen who laughed at wind and waves, and Brian kissed the hand of the

Bird Daughter as he stepped aboard, with never a thought of the storm of men that was coming down upon them both, and of the blacker storm which the Dark Master was brewing in his heart.

CHAPTER VIII

HOW BRIAN WAS NETTED

THE DARK Master sat in his dark hall, brooding.

It was a bad morning, for there was a sweep of wind and black cloud mingled with snow bearing out of the north; and since the great hall, with its huge fireplace, was the warmest part of the castle, as many of the men as could do so had drifted thither, but without making any undue disturbance over it.

For that matter, they might have passed unseen, since the hall was black as night save for a single cresset above the fireplace. Here sat the Dark Master, a little oaken table before him on which his breakfast had rested, and at his side crouched a long, lean wolfhound that nuzzled him unheeded. On the other side the table sat the old *seanachie,* who was blind, and who fingered the strings of his harp with odd twangings and mutterings, but without coherence, for O'Donnell had bade him keep silence.

"Go and see what the weather is," commanded the Dark Master. A man rose and ran outside, while other men came in with wood. Their master motioned them away, although the fire had sunk down into embers.

"A gale from the north, which is turning to the eastward, with snow, master."

"Remain outside, and bring me word what changes hap, and of all that you see or hear. Waste no time about it."

The Dark Master drew his cloak about his humped shoulders, and in the flickering dim light from overhead his face stood out in all its ghastly pallor, accentuated by the dead black hair and mustache. But his eyes were burning strangely, and when they saw it the men drew back, and more than one sought the outer chill in preference to staying.

Now O'Donnell Dubh stared into the embers and muttered below his breath, while, as if in response, a little flickering whirlwind of gray ash rose up and fell back again, so that it blew over the embers and deadened them. The muscles of the Dark Master's face contracted until his teeth flashed out in a silent snarl.

"I could have slain, and I did not," he whispered as if to himself. "But there is still time, and I will not be a fool again!"

The watching men shivered, for it seemed that the wind scurried down the wide chimney and again blew up the gray ash until the embers glowed through a white coating. But the wind wrought more than this, for it brought down from the gray clouds a whispering murmur that drifted through the hall, and in that murmur were mingled the sounds of beating hoofs and ringing steel and shrieking men.

"Are watchers posted over the hills and the paths and the Galway roads?" spoke out the Dark Master as he gazed into the ashes.

"They are watching, master," answered a deep voice from the darkness.

Suddenly the wolfhound raised its head and stared into the ashes also, as if it saw something there that no man saw, for the bristles lifted on its neck, and it whined a little. O'Donnell dropped his hand to the thin muzzle, and the dog was quiet again. But after that the men stared at the fireplace with frightened eyes.

"There is still time, though one has escaped me," said the Dark Master, looking up suddenly at his sightless harper, who seemed to fall atrembling beneath the look. "The one who has escaped matters not, for his bane comes not at my hands. It is the other whom I shall slay—Brian Buidh of the hard eyes. Then the Bird Daughter. But it seems to me that one stands in my path of whom I do not know."

He brooded over the ashes as his head sank between his shoulders like a turtle's head. Then once again the wind swooped down on the castle, and whistled down the chimney, and filled the great hall with a thin noise like the death-rattle of men. The cresset wavered and fell to smoking overhead.

The Dark Master reached his hand across the table and caught the hand of the blind harper and spread it out on the oak. A little shudder shook the old man, and as if against his will he spread out his other hand likewise, his two hands lying between those of the Dark Master. Then there fell a terrible and awestruck silence on the hall.

The stillness was perfect, and continued for a long while. Slowly occurred a weird and strange thing, for, although no blast whimpered down the chimney, the ashes fell away from the embers, which began to glow more redly and set out the forms of the Dark Master and the blind harper in a ruddy light. Suddenly a man pointed to the feet of the Dark Master, and would have cried out but that another man struck him back.

For the ashes had drifted out from the fireplace, flake after flake, and were settling about the feet of the Dark Master beneath the table. They rose slowly into a little gray pile; then one of the men shrieked in horror at the sight, and the Dark Master threw out his head.

"Slay him," he said quietly and drew in his head once more, staring at the table.

There was a thudding blow and a groan, then the stillness of death. The ashes were quiet; the fire glowed ruddily. After a little there came a soft whirl of soot down the chimney, blackening the embers. The soot rose and fell, rose and fell, again and again; it was as if an eddying draft of wind were trying to raise it. Finally it was lifted, but it only whirled about and about over the embers, like a shape drawn together by some uncanny force.

The Dark Master raised his head as a clash of steel and the voice of the watcher came from the outer doorway.

"Master, the blast thickens with black fog!"

"Remain on watch," said O'Donnell, and his head fell.

But through the hall men's hands went out to one another in the darkness. For storm-driven fog was not a thing that many men had seen even on the west coast, and when it did happen men said that a warlock was at work. There was not far to seek for the warlock in this case, muttered the O'Donnells.

Now the Dark Master looked into the fireplace and that whirling figure of soot raised itself anew and began its unearthly dance over the embers. After no long time men saw that the pile of gray ashes under the table was lifting also, lifting and whirling as though the wind spun it; but there was no wind.

"There is a man to be blinded," said the Dark Master. "Let him be blinded with fog and snow, and the men with him, and let the wind come out of the east and drive him to this place."

Slowly, so slowly that no man could afterward say where there was beginning or end, the whirling figure of soot dissipated; and little by little the dancing stream of gray ashes drifted back into the fireplace; then it also dissipated, seeming to pass up the chimney, so that the embers glowed red and naked.

"*Seanachie,*" said the Dark Master in a terribly piercing voice, "who is this standing in my way, standing between me and Brian of the hard eyes?"

The blind harper began to tremble, but again came the clash and the watcher's voice from the doorway.

"Master, there is snow mingled with the fog, and the wind is shifting to the eastward."

"Light the beacon and remain on watch," said the Dark Master. But at the watcher's word new terror seized on the men in the hall.

"*Seanachie,* who stands in my way? Speak!"

The beard of the blind harper quivered and rose as if the wind lifted it, but men felt no wind through the hall. Then the old man began to writhe in his chair, and twisted to take his hands from the table, but he could not, although only he alone held them there. Suddenly his mouth opened, and a voice that was not his voice made answer:

"Master, two people stand in your way."

"Describe them," said the Dark Master, and those near by saw that sweat was running down his face, despite the coldness of the hall. After a moment's silence the old harper spoke again; he had lost his eyes twenty years since, yet he spoke of seeing.

"Master, I see two people but dimly. One is a man, huge of stature and standing like Laeg the hero, the friend of the hero Cuculain, leaning upon an ax—"

"That is Cathbarr of the Ax," broke in the Dark Master. "His bane comes not at my hands. Who is the other?"

Again the old harper seemed to struggle, and his voice came more faintly:

"I cannot see, master. I think it is a woman—"

"That is the Bird Daughter," quoth the Dark Master.

"Nay, it is an old woman, but she blinds me—"

And the harper fell silent, writhing, until horror gripped those who looked on. O'Donnell leaned forward, his head sticking straight out and his eyes blazing.

"What do you see, *seanachie?* Speak!"

"I see men," and the old harper's voice rose in a great shriek. "A storm of men and of hoofs, and red snow on the ground, and fire over the snow, and the man of the ax laughing terribly. And I see other men riding hard; men with long hair and the flag of England in their midst—and Cuculain smites them—Cuculain of the yellow hair—the Royal Hound of Ulster smites them and scatters them—"

"*Liar!*"

With the hoarse word the Dark Master leaned forward and smote the blind harper with his fist, so that the old man slid from his chair senseless. Upon that the Dark Master swung around with his teeth bared and his head drawn in like the head of a snake about to strike.

"Lights!" he roared. "Lights! Bear the *seanachie* to his chamber, and send men to ring in the harbor and build beacons on the headlands. Hasten, you dogs, or I'll strip the flesh from you with whips!"

Under his voice and his flaming eyes the hall sprang into life, while the men carried out the blind harper and one of their own number who had been stricken with madness at what he had seen. Then the hall blazed up with cressets, logs were flung on the fire, and parties of men set out to build beacons and guard the bay as the Dark Master had given command. And when word was spread abroad among the others of what had chanced in the hall that morning, Red Murrough, the Dark Master's lieutenant, swore a great oath.

"If that Cuculain of whom the *seanachie* spoke be not the man Brian Buidh, then may I go down to hell alive!"

And the men, who feared Red Murrough's heavy hand and hated him, muttered that he would be like to travel that same road whether living or dead, in which there was some truth.

While these things took place in the hall at Bertragh—and they were told later to Brian by many who had seen them and heard them, all telling the same tale—Brian and his sailing galley was making hard weather of it. Six of the O'Malleys had been sent with him to manage the galley, for he was no seaman and had placed himself in their hands; and after rounding into Kilkieran Bay from the castle harbor and reaching out across the mouth of the bay toward Carna, intending to reach Cathbarr's tower direct, the blast came down on them, and even the O'Malleys looked stern.

Sterner yet they looked when Brian cried that Golam Head was veiling in fog behind them, and with that the wind swerved almost in a moment and swept down out of the east, bearing fog and snow with it. Nor was this all, for the shift of wind bore against the seas and swept down currents and whirlpools out of the bay, and after the snow and black fog shrieked down upon them, the seamen straightway fell to praying.

"Get up and bail!" shouted Brian, kicking them to their feet, for the seas were sweeping over the counter. The helmsman groaned and bade him desist, and almost at the same instant their mast crashed over the bow, breaking the back of one seaman, and the galley broached to.

With that the O'Malleys ceased praying and fell to work with a will, getting out the sweeps and bailing. The mingling of snow, shrieking wind, and black fog had been too much for their superstitious natures, but made no impression on Brian, for the simple reason that he did not see why fog and wind should not come together. After he understood their fears better he shamed them into savage energy by his laughter, and since the broken-backed man had gone overboard, took his sweep and set his muscles to work.

They made shift to keep the craft before the wind, but presently Brian found that half the men's fear sprang from the fact that the fog and snow blinded them, shutting out the land, and that the shifting wind had completely bewildered them. When he asked for their compass, their leader grunted:

"No need have we for a compass on this boat, Brian Buidh, save when warlocks turn the fog and wind upon us. I warrant that were it not for the fog, we would be safe in port ere now. As it is, the Virgin alone knows where we are or whither going."

"This is some of the Dark Master's wizardry," growled out another. "Before we hung those men of his last night, they said that the winds would bear word of it to the dark one, *cead mile mollaght* on him!"

"Add another thousand curses for me," ordered Brian, "but keep to the bailing, or I'll give you a taste of my foot! And no more talk of warlocks."

The five men fell silent, and indeed they needed all their breath, for the struggle was a desperate one. Instead of lessening, the fog only increased with time, and even Brian began to perceive the marvel in it as swirl after swirl of darkness swept over them. Yet, since the wind was from the east, he reasoned, it would naturally blow out the fog from the bogs and low lands. But this explanation was received in dour silence by the men, so he said no more.

There was no doubt that Cathbarr had reached home safely, since the night had been fair enough for the winter season. An hour passed, and then another, still without a lessening of the eery storm; and the nerve of the seamen was beginning to give way under the strain, when the helmsman let out a wild yell:

"A light ahead! A beacon!"

The rowers twisted about with shouts of joy, and Brian perceived a faint, ruddy light against the sky. Also, the fog began to lessen somewhat; and upon making out that the beacon undoubtedly came from a high tower or crag, the shout passed around that they had headed back to Gorumna with the shifting wind.

This heartened them all greatly, the more so since the gale drove them straight onward toward the beacon. The fog closed down again, but the ruddy glare pierced through it; and of a sudden there was no more fog about them—only a blinding thick snow, which made all things grotesque. Then two more beacons were made out, lower than the first, and the men yelled joyously that fires had been lighted on either side the harbor to guide them in. And so they had been, but otherwise than the men thought.

Half frozen with the cold, they drove on through the snow and spray until at length they swept in between the guiding fires and scanned the shores for landing. Then the snow ceased, though the hurricane howled down behind them with redoubled fury; and as they floated in against a low, rocky shore, silence of wild consternation fell on them all. For they had come to Bertragh Castle, and fifty feet away a score of men were waiting, while others were running down with torches.

Even in that moment of terrible dismay, Brian noted their

muskets, and how the lighted matches flared like fireflies in the wind.

"Trapped!" groaned one of the men, and they would have rowed out again into the teeth of the storm had not Brian stayed them.

"No use, comrades. They have muskets, and there are cannon up above. Row in, and if we must die, then let us die like men and not cowards."

Seeing no help for it, the men growled assent, and they drifted slowly in, all standing ready with drawn swords, while Brian's Spanish blade flared in the prow. Then in the midst of the gathered men he saw a dark figure with hunched shoulders, sword in hand. As he turned to the seamen behind him, there was a glitter in his blue eyes colder than the icy blast behind them.

"There is the Dark Master, comrades! Let him be first to fall."

They drove up on the shore, and Brian leaped out, with the men behind him. Still the group above stood silent until the voice of O'Donnell sheared through the gale. "Fire, and drop Yellow Brian first."

So there was to be no word of quarter! As the thought shot like fire through Brian's mind, he leaped forward with a shout. A ragged stream of musketry broke out from the men gathered on the higher rocks, and he heard the bullets whistle. He paid no heed to the seamen who followed him, however. His eyes were fixed on the Dark Master's figure, and with only one thought in his mind he plunged ahead.

More and more muskets spattered out; a bullet splashed against his jack, and another; something caught his steel cap and tore it away, and a hot stab shot through his neck. But the group of men was only a dozen paces from him now, and a wild yell broke from his lips as he saw O'Donnell step forward to meet him.

Then only did he remember Turlough's speech on the day of that first meeting with the Dark Master—"The master of all men at craft and the match of most men at weapons"—and he knew that, despite the hunched shoulders, this O'Donnell must be no mean fighter. But the next instant he was gazing into the evil eyes, and their blades had crossed.

Flaming with his anger, Brian forced the attack savagely; then a sharp thrust against his jack showed him that O'Donnell was armed with a rapier, and he fell to the point with some caution. With the first moment of play, he knew that he faced a master of fence; yet almost upon the thought his blade ripped into the Dark Master's arm.

Involuntarily he drew back, but O'Donnell caught the falling sword in his left hand and lunged forward viciously. Just as the blades met again, Brian saw a match go to a musket barely six paces away. He whirled aside, but too late, for the musket roared out, and a drift of stars poured into his brain. Then he fell.

Like a flash the Dark Master leaped at the man who had fired and spitted him through the throat; the others drew back in swift terror, for O'Donnell was frothing at the mouth, and his face was the face of a madman. With a bitter laugh he turned and rolled Brian over with his foot. The five seamen had gone down under the bullets.

"He is only stunned," said Red Murrough. "Shall I finish it?"

"If you want to die with him, yes. Carry him in, and we will nail him up to the gates to-morrow."

And the clouds fell asunder, and the stars came out, cold and beautiful.

CHAPTER IX

THE NAILING OF BRIAN

BRIAN WOKE in darkness, with pain tearing at his head and heaviness upon his hands and feet. When he tried to put his hand to his head, that heaviness was explained; for he could not, and thick iron struck dull against stone.

He lay there, and thought leaped into his brain, and he felt very bitter of spirit, but chiefly for those men who had come with him, and because he had failed before the Dark Master's hand.

It was cold, bitterly cold, and thin snow lay around him, so that he knew that he was in some tower or prison that faced to the east. It was from that direction that the snow had driven, as he had sore cause to know, and he wondered if the Dark Master had had any hand in that driving. But this he was not to know for many days.

It was the cold which had awakened him from his unconsciousness, he guessed. By dint of shifting his position somewhat, he managed to get his back against a wall, and so got his hands to his head. In such fashion he made out that his hair was matted and frozen with blood, and his neck also, where a bullet had plowed through the muscles on the right side. His headwound was no more than a jagged tear which had split half his scalp, but had not hurt the bone, as he found after some feeling. Then he dropped his hands again, for the chains that bound him to the wall were very heavy. It must be night, for light would come where snow had come, and there was no light.

Now, having found that he was not like to die, at least from his wounds, he set about stretching to lie down again, and found some straw on the floor. He drew it up with his feet and gathered it about him; it was dank and smelled vilely, but at the least it gave his frozen body some warmth, so that he fell asleep after a time.

When he wakened again, it was to find men around him and a narrow strip of cold sunlight coming through a high slit in the wall of his prison. From the sound of breakers that seemed to roar from below him, he conjectured that he was in a sea-facing tower of the castle, in which he was right.

The men, who were led by Red Murrough, gave him bread and meat and wine, but they offered no word and would answer no questions. So he ate and drank, and felt life and strength creeping back into his bones. He concluded that it must be the day after his arrival.

Now Red Murrough beckoned to the hoary old seneschal, whose red-rimmed eyes glittered evilly. The old man shook his keys and stooped over Brian, unlocking the hasp which bound him to the wall-ring. The oppressive silence of these men struck a chill through Brian, but he came to his feet readily enough as Murrough jerked his shoulder.

He followed out into a corridor, and the men closed around him, going with him down-stairs and along other passageways. Brian wondered as to his fate and what manner of death he was going to die; yet it seemed to him that death was an impossible and far-off thing where he was concerned.

He expected no less than death from the Dark Master, but at the same time it was very hard to believe that he was going to that fate. He was by no means afraid to die, but he felt that he would like to see the Bird Daughter once more. Also, he had always thought of fate as coming to him suddenly and swiftly in battle or foray; and to be deliberately done to death in cold blood by hanging or otherwise was not as he would have wished.

"At least," he thought without any great comfort, "Cathbarr

and Turlough will avenge me on the Dark Master—though I had liefer be living when that was done!"

In one of the larger and lower corridors they came on two men bearing a body, sewed for burial. Murrough stopped his party and growled out something.

"It is the *seanachie*," answered one of the bearers. "Since the Dark Master struck him yester-morn he has not spoken, and he died last night."

Upon this Red Murrough crossed himself, as did the rest, muttered into his tangle of red beard, and motioned Brian forward.

This wider passage gave through a doorway upon the great hall. There was no dais, but the Dark Master was seated before the huge fireplace, his wolf-hound crouched down at his side. The hall was pierced near the roof with openings, and lower down with loopholes, so that when the sun shone outside it was bright enough.

Red Murrough led Brian forward, the clank of the heavy chain-links echoing hollowly through the place, but O'Donnell Dubh did not look up until the two men stood a scant four paces from him. Then his head came out from between his rounded shoulders and his eyes spat fire at Brian.

"A poor ending to proud talk, Brian Buidh!"

Brian tried to smile, but with ill success, for he was chilled to the bone and there was blood on his face.

"I am not yet dead, O'Donnell."

"You will be soon enough," the Dark Master chuckled, and the hall thrilled with evil laughter. In the eyes of all Brian had proven himself the weaker man and therefore deserved his fate. "What of this O'Malley journey of yours, eh?"

Brian made no answer, save that his strong lips clamped shut, and his blue eyes narrowed a little. O'Donnell laughed and began to stroke his wolf-hound.

"I have many messengers and many servants, Yellow Brian, and there is little my enemies do which is not told me. Even now men are riding hard and fast to trap Cathbarr of the Ax and your following."

At that Brian laughed, remembering Turlough Wolf and his cunning.

"I think this trapping will prove a hard matter, Dark Master."

"That is as it may be. Now, Brian Buidh, death is hard upon you, and neither an easy nor a swift one. Before you die there are two things which I would know from your lips."

Brian looked at him, but without speaking. The Dark Master had thrust out his head, his hand still lingering on the wolf-hound's neck, and his pallid face, drooping mustache, and high brow were very evil to gaze upon. Brian, eying that thin-nostriled, cruel nose, and the undershot jaw of the man, read no mercy there.

"First, who *are* you, Brian Buidh? Are you an O'Neill, as that ring of yours would testify, or are you an O'Malley come down from the western isles?"

At that Brian laughed out harshly. "Ask those servants of which you boast, Dark Master. Poor they must be if they cannot tell you even the names of your enemies!"

"Well answered!" grinned the other, and chuckled again to himself as though the reply had indeed pleased him hugely. "I would that you served me, Brian of the hard eyes; I suppose that you are some left-hand scion of the Tyr-owens by some woman overseas, and the O'Neill bastards were ever as strong in arm as the true sons. Yet you might have made pact with me, whereas now your head shall sit on my gates, after your bones are broken and you have been nailed to a door."

"Fools talk over-much of killing, but wise men smite first and talk after," Brian said contemptuously. He saw that the Dark Master was somewhat in doubt over slaying him, since if he were indeed an O'Neill there might be bitter vengeance looked for, or if he belonged to any other of the great families.

"Quite true," countered the Dark Master mockingly, and with much relish. "Therein you were a fool, not to slay when first we met, instead of making pacts. Who will repay me my two-score men, Brian of the hollow cheeks?"

"The Bird Daughter, perhaps," smiled Brian, "since two days ago she hung ten of those men I took in my ambuscade."

This stung O'Donnell, and his men with him. One low, deep growl swirled down the hall, and the Dark Master snarled as his lips bared back from his teeth. Brian laughed out again, standing very tall and straight, and his chains clanked a little and stilled the murmur. He saw that O'Donnell wore his own Spanish blade, and the sight angered him.

"There is another thing I would know," said the Dark Master slowly. "Tell me this thing, Brian Buidh, and I will turn you out of my gates a free man."

Brian looked keenly at him and saw that the promise was given in earnest. He wondered what the thing might be, and was not long in learning.

"You came hither from Gorumna Castle," went on O'Donnell, fixing him with his black flaming eyes. "Tell me what force of men is in that place, Brian of the hard eyes, and for this service you shall be set free."

"Now I know that you are a fool, O'Donnell Dubh," and Brian's voice rang out merrily. "I have heard many tales of your wizardry and your servants and your watchers, but when an unknown man comes to you, his name is hidden from you; and all your black art cannot so much as tell you the number of your enemies! Now slay me and have done, for you have wasted much breath this day, and so have I, and it goes ill in my mind to waste speech on fools."

"You refuse then?" O'Donnell peered up at him, but Brian set his face hard and made no reply. With a little sigh the Dark Master leaned back in his chair and motioned to Red Murrough to come forward.

"Strip him," he said evenly, and at the word a great howl rang out from all the watching men, like the howl of wolves when they scent blood in the air.

Murrough in turn signed to two of his men. These came forward and stripped off what clothes had been left to Brian, so that he stood naked before them. In that moment he was minded to spring on the Dark Master and crush him with his chains, but he saw that Red Murrough held a flint-lock pistolet cocked, and knew it would be useless. Also, if he had to die, he was minded to do it like a man and not to shame the blood of Tyr-owen, either by seeking death or by shrinking at its face.

Now there passed a murmur through the hall, and even the Dark Master's evil features glowed a little; for Brian's body was very fair and slim and white, yet these judges of men saw that he was like a thing of steel, and that beneath the satin skin his body was all rippling sinew. Red Murrough drew out a hasp, brought his chained hands together, and caught the chain close to his wrists, so that his hands were bound close.

"Now," said the Dark Master, settling back and stroking his wolfhound as if he were watching some curious spectacle, "do with him as we did with Con O'More last Candlemas. But let us work slowly, for there is no haste, and we must break his will. In the end we will nail him to the door, and finish by breaking all his bones. It will be very interesting, eh?"

A fierce howl and clash of steel answered him from the men. At another sign from Red Murrough, Brian felt himself jerked to the floor suddenly, and his hands were drawn up over his head. His wrist-chains were fastened to an iron ring set in the floor, and his ankles to another, and he stared up at the ceiling-rafters of the hall, watching the motes drift past overhead in the reaching sunbeams. It all seemed very unreal to him.

"First that long hair of his," said the Dark Master quietly.

Murrough went to the fire and returned with a blazing stick. Brian's gold-red hair had flung back from his head, along the floor, and presently he felt it burning, until his head was scorched and his brain began to roast and there was the smell of burnt hair rising from him. Then Murrough's rough hand brushed over his torn scalp, quelling the fire, but it did not quell the agony that wrenched Brian.

"Paint him," ordered O'Donnell.

Again Murrough went to the fireplace, and returned with a long white-hot iron which had lain among the embers. This he touched to Brian's right shoulder, so that the stench of scorched flesh sizzled up in a thin stream, and followed the iron down across the white breast and thigh, until it stopped at the knee, and there was a swath of red and blackened flesh down Brian's body. Yet he had not moved or flinched.

Then Murrough touched the iron to his left shoulder and drew it very slowly down his left side. One of the watching men went sick with the smell and went out vomiting. A second swath of red and black rose on the white flesh, and beneath it all Brian felt his senses swirling. Try as he would he could not repress one long shudder, at which a wild yell of delight shrilled up—and then he fainted.

"Take him away," said the Dark Master, smiling a little, as he leaned forward and saw that Brian had indeed swooned with the pain. "To-morrow we will paint his back with the whip."

So they loosened him from the iron rings, and four men lifted him and carried him out. As they passed across the courtyard another came by with a pail of sea-water, which they flung over him; the salt entered into his wounds, washing away the blackness from his scalp, and slowly the life came back to him after he had been chained again in his tower-room and left alone.

He was sorry for this, because he thought that he had died under the iron. He found a pitcher of water beside him, and after drinking a little he spent the rest in washing out the salt from his flesh, though every motion was terrible in its torture. So great was the pain that gasping sobs shook him, though he stared up dry-eyed at the stones, and a great desire for death came upon him.

"Slay me, oh God!" he groaned, shuddering again in his anguish. "Slay me, for I am helpless and cannot slay myself!"

As if in answer, there came a soft laugh from somewhere overhead, and the voice of the Dark Master.

"There is no God in Bertragh Castle save O'Donnell, Brian Buidh!"

The blasphemy shocked him into his senses, which had wandered. Now he knew that from some hidden place the Dark Master was watching him and listening for his ravings, and upon that Brian sternly caught his lips together and said no more, though he prayed hard within himself. A cloak had been laid near-by him, and when he had covered himself somewhat against the cold, though with great pain in the doing, he lay quiet.

The cold crept into him and for a space he was seized with chills that sent new thrills of pain through his burned body, for he could not repress them. After a time he relapsed slowly into numbed unconsciousness, waking from time to time, and so the hours dragged away until the night came.

Then men brought him more food and wine and straw, and he managed to sleep a bit during the darkness, in utmost misery. But after the day had come, and more wine had stirred his blood redly, Murrough fetched him to his feet and bade him follow. Brian did it, though walking was agony, for his pride was stronger even than his torture.

He was halted in the courtyard, found the Dark Master and his men gathered there, and knew that more torture was to come upon him. After a single scornful glance the Dark Master ordered him triced up to a post, which was done. Brian saw a man standing by with a long whip, but gained a brief respite as the drawbridge was lowered to admit a messenger mounted on a shaggy hill-pony. O'Donnell bade him make haste with his errand.

"The word has come, master, that five hundred of Lord Burke's pikemen are on the road from Galway and will be close by within a day or so."

"And what of Cathbarr of the Ax?" queried the Dark Master.

Brian's heart caught at the words, then his head fell again at the response.

"They have scattered in the mountains, it is said, master."

"Murrough, have men sent to meet these royalists with food and wines, and if they are bound hither we will entreat them softly and send them home again empty. Now let us enjoy Brian Buidh a while—though he has stood up but poorly. It is in my mind that we will nail him up to-morrow."

With that Brian felt the whip stroking across his naked back. His muscles corded and heaved up in horrible contraction, but no sound broke from him; again and again the hide whip licked about him until he felt the warm blood running down his legs, and then with merciful suddenness all things went black, and he hung limp against the post.

"Take him back," ordered the Dark Master in disgust. "Why, that boy we cut up the other side of Clifden had more strength than this fool!"

"His strength went out of him with his hair," grinned Red Murrough, and they carried Brian to his prison.

The Dark Master had spoken truly, however. Brian's strength lay not so much in brute muscles, though he had enough of them, as in his nervous energy; and the slow horror of his burning hair and of that iron which had twice raked the length of his body had come close to destroying his whole nervous system. Other men might have endured the same thing and laughed the next day, but Brian was high-strung and tense, and while his will was still strong, his physical endurance was shattered.

With the next morning, this fact had become quite evident to the general disgust of all within Bertragh Castle. The Dark Master himself visited the cell, and upon finding that Brian was lost in a half stupor and muttering words in Spanish which no one understood, he angrily ordered that he be revived and finished with that afternoon.

Red Murrough set about the task with savage determination. By dint of sea water externally and mingled wine and uisquebagh internally he had Brian wakened to a semblance of himself before midday. Then food, oil, and bandages about his wounds, and in another hour Brian was feeling like a new man.

He was under no misapprehension as to the cause of this kindness, but cared little. So keenly had he suffered that he was glad to reach the end, and he walked out behind Red Murrough that afternoon with a ghastly face, but with firm mouth and firmer stride, though he was very weak and half-drunk with the liquors he had swallowed.

His fetters were unlocked and he was led to the doorway of the great hall, with the Dark Master and his men watching eagerly. Red Murrough, with an evil grin, pressed his back to the door and held up his left arm against the heavy wood. Brian was half-conscious of another man who bore a heavy mallet and spikes, and whose breath came foul on his face as he pressed something cold against the extended left hand.

Then Brian saw the mallet swing back, heard a sickening crunch, and with a terrible pain shooting to his soul, fell asleep.

CHAPTER X

IN BERTRAGH CASTLE

NOW, OF what befell after that nail had been driven through his hand, Brian learned afterward; though at the time he was unconscious and seemed like to remain so. Hardly had he sagged forward limply when two men came riding up to the gates demanding instant admittance. One of these was of the Dark Master's band, the other was a certain Colonel James Vere, of the garrison which held Galway for the king.

O'Donnell, who suddenly found himself with greater things on hand than the nailing of a prisoner, ordered Brian left where he lay for the present, and had the drawbridge lowered in all haste. Colonel Vere, who had late been in rebellion against his gracious majesty, was now joined with Ormond's men against the common enemy, and was in command of that force of five hundred pikemen which had been marching to the west.

Knowing this, the Dark Master made ready to set his house in order, since it was known that Vere's men were only a few hours away. Hardly had the garrison gone to their posts, leaving Brian in the center of a little group about the hall doorway, when Colonel Vere rode in and was received in as stately fashion as possible by the Dark Master. It was not for nothing that O'Donnell had trimmed his sails to the blast, since he was on very good terms with all in Galway.

"Welcome," he exclaimed with a low bow as Vere swung down from his saddle. "Your men received the provision I sent off yesterday?"

"Aye, and thankful we were!" cried the other cheerily, for he was a red-faced man of forty, a Munsterman and half-English, and loved his bottle. "Hearing certain news from one of your men I made bold to ride ahead in all haste, O'Donnell."

"News?" repeated the Dark Master softly. "And of what nature, Colonel Vere?"

"Why, of one Brian Buidh, or Yellow Brian." At this the Dark Master began to finger the Spanish blade he had taken from Brian, and for a second Vere was very near to death, had he known it.

"What of him, Colonel Vere?"

"Why, the rogue had the impudence to come down on a convoy of powder and stores, last week, going from the Archbishop at Ennis to Malbay, for our use. Not only this, but a hundred of our rascally Scots deserted to him, he slipped past us at Galway, and I was in hopes you could give me word of him when I hit over this way. You're something of a ravager yourself, sink me if you aren't!" and he dug the Dark Master jovially in the ribs.

"Yes," murmured O'Donnell thoughtfully, "so they say, Colonel Vere. But only when Parliament men come past, you understand. So you heard that this Yellow Brian was here?"

"Aye, and that you were doing him to death," coolly responded Vere, and his eyes flickered to the white form on the stones. "Zounds! What's this?"

"Yellow Brian," responded the Dark Master dryly. "What do you want with him?"

"Eh? Why, I'll take him back to Galway and hang him! I've a dozen of the Scots he was fool enough to let loose, and when my men come up they'll identify him readily enough."

"Unless he's dead," chuckled O'Donnell. "Well, if you want him you may have him and welcome. So now come in and sample some prime sack I took from the O'Malleys last year."

"With all the honors," responded Vere gallantly, and as they strode past Brian the Dark Master hastily directed that he be washed and tended and brought back to his right mind as soon as might be.

This order, and the conversation preceding it, gave Red Murrough some cause for thought. So it was that when Brian wakened once more in his cell, as evening was falling, he found the fetters on him indeed, but Red Murrough had bound up his wounds, dressed his sundered hand-bones, and was sitting watching him reflectively. It had occurred to the Dark Master's lieutenant that there might be something made out of this man, who seemed wanted in several places at once.

Therefore it was that while Brian made an excellent meal for a man swathed from crown to knees in bandages, Red Murrough poured into his ear the tale of what had chanced in the court-yard, and why it was that he was not at this moment nailed to the castle door. Brian collected his energy with some effort.

"Well, what of it?" he asked weakly.

"Just this, Yellow Brian," and Murrough stroked his matted red beard easily. "O'Donnell will make a good thing out of hand-ing you over to the royalists, who mean to hang you in style, it seems. Now, it is in my mind that it might advantage you some-what if you were not moved thence for a few days—indeed, you might even escape, for I think you are not without friends."

"Eh?" Brian stared up at him wonderingly. "What does it matter to you?"

"Nothing, whether you live or die. But you are in my care, and if I report that you are in too bad shape to be moved—which you are not—then this Colonel Vere will camp outside our castle until you are handed over to him. You will gain a few days in which to get your wits back, and the rest is in your hands."

"I had not thought you loved me so much," and despite his agony Brian forced out a bitter laugh.

"Not I! Faith, I had liefer see you nailed—but a service may be paid for."

"I have no money," Brian closed his eyes wearily.

"No, but you have friends," and Murrough leaned forward.

"Promise me a clerkly writing to the Bird Daughter's men, or to your own men, ordering that I be paid ten English pounds, and it is done."

"With pleasure," smiled Brian wryly. "Also, if I escape, I will spare your life one day, Red Murrough."

"Good. Then play your part." And Murrough departed well pleased with his acumen.

And indeed, the man carried out his bargain more than faithfully. One visit assured the Dark Master that this broken, burned, cloth-swathed man was helpless to harm him further, and after that he gave Brian little thought.

As Murrough had reckoned Brian's swoop on the convoy had given him some notoriety, and more than once Brian himself remembered Cathbarr's dark presage after he had let the ten Scots go free to Ennis; Colonel Vere was anxious to carry him back to Galway for an example to other freebooters, and he was quite content to bide at Bertragh Castle until his prisoner could travel.

For that matter the other officers of his command were quite as content as he himself, since all were men from the south-country who loved good wines, and the Dark Master had better store of these than the empty royalist commissariat.

As for the Dark Master, Murrough reported to Brian that he also was well content. Cromwell was sweeping like an avenging flame from Kilkenny to Mallow and Ormond was helpless before him; both king's men and Irish Confederacy men were pouring out of the South in despair, but the two had finally joined forces and the final stand would take place in the West. In fact, it seemed that things were dark for Parliament, despite Cromwell's activity, and the Dark Master was only one of many such who counted strongly on the rumors that the new king, Charles II, was on his way to Ireland with aid from France.

And indeed he was at that time; but Charles, then and later, was more apt at starting a thing than at finishing it.

Red Murrough lost no time in getting his "clerkly writing,"

luckily for himself. On the morning after his agreement he brought Brian a quill, and blood for lack of ink, and sheepskin. Brian wrote the order for ten pounds, promising to honor it himself if he escaped.

This, however, did not seem likely, and even Murrough frankly stated that it was impossible. But Brian was tended well, and his perfect health was a strong asset. His head had been little more than scorched, and the scalp-wound stayed clean; after the first day there came a festering in his broken hand, but Murrough washed it out with vinegar which ate out the wound and cleansed it, after which he bound it firmly in wooden splints and it promised well.

More than once Brian laughed grimly at the care he was getting, to the simple end that he should hang over Galway gates as a warning to the City of the Tribes and to all who entered the ancient Connacian town. For in that day Galway was a second Venice, and its commerce made rich plundering for the O'Malley's both of Gorumna and of Erris in the North, though the war had somewhat dimmed the glory of the fourteen great merchant families.

Brian wondered often what had become of Cathbarr and his two hundred men, and Murrough could give him little satisfaction. It was known that the force had slipped away from Cathbarr's tower and had vanished; Brian guessed that Turlough had either led them north, or else into the western mountains where the O'Flahertys held savage rule. However, it was certain that neither the Dark Master nor the royalists had scattered them as yet.

So Brian lay in his tower four days and might have lain there four-score more by dint of Red Murrough's lies, had it not been that on the fourth evening Colonel Vere managed to stay unexpectedly sober. Being thus sober, it occurred to him that he had best make sure he had the right man by the heels. So he ordered his ten Scots troopers in from the camp outside the walls, and the Dark Master sent for Brian to be identified.

"I'll have you carried down," said Red Murrough on coming for him. "Play the part, *ma boucal,* and when these royalists get into their cups again they'll forget all that is in their heads. Here's a cup of wine before ye go, and another for myself. *Slainte!"*

"Slainte," repeated Brian, and went forth to play his part.

When the four men, with Red Murrough at their head, carried him down into the great hall, Brian found it no little changed. Tables were set along the walls, each of them being some ten feet in length by two wide, of massive oak, and in the center was another at which sat O'Donnell, Colonel Vere, and one or two other officers. Besides these there were a score more of the royalist officers mingled with the Dark Master's men, and it seemed that there would be few sober men in that hall by midnight, from the appearance of things. Only the ten Scots stood calm and dour before the fireplace.

After that first quick glance around, Brian lay with his head back and his eyes closed, careful not to excite O'Donnell's suspicion that he was stronger than he seemed. He was set down in front of the ten Scots, and there was an eager craning forward of men to look at him, for his name was better known than himself.

"Zounds!" swore Vere thickly. "The man has a strong and clean-cut face, O'Donnell! Strike me dead if he does not look like that painting of O'Neill, the Tyrone Earl, that hangs in the castle at Dublin! Though for that matter there is little enough of his face to be seen. You must have borne hardly on him with your cursed tortures."

"I fancy he is an O'Neill bastard," returned the Dark Master lightly. Brian felt the red creep into his face, but he knew that he was helpless in his chains, and he lay quiet. "Is he your man, Vere?"

"How the devil should I know?" Vere turned to the troopers and spoke in English. "Well, boys, is this the fellow we're after? Speak up now!"

"It's no' sae easy tae ken," returned one cautiously. "Yon man has the look o' Brian Buidh, aye."

"Devil take you!" cried Vere irritably. "Do you mean to say yes or no? Speak out, one of you!"

"Weel, Colonel," answered another cannily, "Jock here has the right of it. I wouldna swear tae the pawky carl, but I'd ken the een o' him full weel. An I had a peep in his een, sir. I'm thinkin' I'd ken their de'il's look. Eh, lads?"

Since it seemed agreed that they would know Brian better by his hard blue eyes than by what they could see of his face, the exasperated Vere commanded that he be made open them if he were unconscious.

"Run your hand down his body, Murrough," ordered the Dark Master cynically.

Red Murrough leaned over Brian, and the latter opened his eyes without waiting for the rough command to be obeyed. Instantly the Scots broke into a chorus of recognition as Brian's gaze fell on them. Vere looked at him with an admiring laugh.

"Sink me, but the man has eyes! Well, so much the better for the ladies, eh? Now that this is over, give the lad a rouse and send him back to his cell."

He waved the Scots to begone, and rose cup in hand. Smiling evilly, the Dark Master joined him in the toast to Brian, and a yell of delight broke from the crowd as they caught the jest and joined in. O'Donnell was just motioning Murrough to have Brian taken away, when there came a sudden interruption, as a man hastened up the hall. It was one of Vere's pikemen.

"There is a party of four horsemen just outside our camp, colonel. One of them bade us get safe-conduct for him from O'Donnell Dubh, upon his honor."

"Eh?" the Dark Master snarled suddenly. "What was his name, fool?"

"Cathbarr of the Ax, lord."

A thrill shot through Brian, and he tried feebly to sit up. The Dark Master flashed him a glance. The hall had fallen silent.

"His business?"

"He bears word from one called the Bird Daughter, he said."

While the royalists stared, wondering what all this boded, O'Donnell bit his lips in thought. Finally he nodded.

"Let the man enter, and tell him that he has my honor for his safe-conduct."

Vere nodded, and the pikeman departed. Instantly the hall broke into uproar, but leaving the table, the Dark Master crossed swiftly to Brian, and bent over him.

"Either swear to keep silence, or I have you gagged."

"I promise," mumbled Brian as if he were very weak. The Dark Master ordered him carried behind one of the tables close by, and a cloak flung over him. When it had been done, Brian found that he could see without being seen, which was the intent of O'Donnell.

Meanwhile the Dark Master was telling Vere and the other officers of Cathbarr, it seemed, and Vere hastily collected his wine-stricken senses.

"Nuala O'Malley, eh?" he exclaimed when the Dark Master had finished. "She is the one who has held Gorumna Castle and would make no treaty with us, though she has more than once sent us powder, I understand."

"I will talk with you later concerning her," returned O'Donnell. "She is allied with Parliament, they say, and it might be well for all of us if ships were sent against her place from Galway, and she were reduced."

Brian saw that things were going badly. The Dark Master seemed to be playing his cards well, and was doubtless thinking of throwing off the cloak and openly allying himself with the royalist cause. In this way he could secure help against Gorumna in the shape of Galway ships and men, and it was like to go hard with the Bird Daughter in such case.

However, Vere had no power to treat of such things, as Brian well knew. Also, Nuala had told him herself that her ships had not preyed on the commerce of Galway's merchants, but only on certain foreign caracks which free-traded along the coast. Therefore the Galwegians were not apt to make a troublesome enemy in haste, even if she were proved to be in alliance with Cromwell.

None the less, the Dark Master was plainly thinking of making an effort in this direction, and Brian knew that the Bird Daughter was in no shape to carry things with a high hand in Galway town.

He saw Vere and the Dark Master talking earnestly together across the table, but could not hear their words—and it was well, indeed, for him that he could not. As he was to find shortly, O'Donnell's quick brain had already grasped at what lay behind Cathbarr's coming, or something of it, and he had formed the devilish scheme on the instant—that scheme which was to result in many things then undreamed of.

"If I had followed Turlough's rede, there when I first met this devil," thought Brian bitterly, "I had slain him upon the road, and that would have been an end of it. Well, I think that I shall heed Turlough Wolf next time—if there is a next time."

Brian looked out from his shelter with troubled eyes, for there was something in the wind of which he had no inkling. He saw Vere break into a sudden coarse laugh, and a great light of evil triumph shot across O'Donnell's face. Then the Dark Master gained his feet, gathered his cloak about his hunched shoulders, and sent Murrough to stand guard over Brian with a pistol and to shoot if he spoke out.

"Surely he cannot be going back on his word, passed before so many men?" thought Brian bitterly. "No, that would shame him before all Galway, and he is proud in his way. But what the devil can be forward?"

To that he obtained no answer. The Dark Master shoved his table back toward the fireplace, and placed his chair in front of it beside that of Colonel Vere. It seemed to Brian that the stage was being set for some grim scene, and a great fear seized on him lest harm was in truth meant toward Cathbarr.

No doubt the giant had been in communication with the Bird Daughter, and it had been ascertained that the galley had come to grief at Bertragh Castle. A sudden thrill of hope darted through Brian. Was it possible that Cathbarr had led down his men and placed them in readiness to attack? Yet such a thing would have been madness—to set a scant two hundred against Vere's pikemen and the Dark Master's force combined!

But Brian knew that Turlough Wolf was at large, and Turlough's brain was more cunning than most.

If he could only get free, he thought, he might still be able to do something. He could ride, though it would mean bitter pain, and his sword-arm was still good—but he had got no farther than this when there came a tramping of feet, and in the doorway appeared Cathbarr, his mighty ax in hand, with the O'Donnells around him as jackals surround a lion.

CHAPTER XI

THE BAITING OF CATHBARR

THE BEARDED giant still wore the long mail-shirt that reached to his knees, and he paused at the doorway with his eyes roving about the hall. Well did Brian know whom he sought, but it was vain, for Cathbarr could not see him where he lay.

Then Brian saw that the ax had been changed, and wondered at it. One of the long, back-curving blades had been rubbed down with files, so that it was very tapering and thin like an ordinary ax-blade, while the other was still the blunt, heavy thing it had always been. Brian read the cunning of Turlough Wolf in that handiwork, and in fact the great ax was thus rendered tenfold more deadly.

The Dark Master waited quietly until Cathbarr began a slow advance up the hall, all eyes fixed on him in no little wonder. Then O'Donnell raised a hand, stopping him.

"Let us have your message, Cathbarr."

The giant halted and dropped the ax-head, leaning on the haft of the weapon. He took his time about replying, however, and his eyes still roved about the hall ceaselessly and uneasily. Then of a sudden he gave over the search, and gazed straight at the Dark Master with a swift word:

"Have you slain him?"

"Slain who, Cathbarr?" queried O'Donnell, with a thin smile.

"Duar na Criosd!" bellowed Cathbarr with sudden fury. "Who but my friend Brian?"

"Oh!" The Dark Master laughed and eased back in his chair. "No, he's still alive, Cathbarr? Is your message from the Bird Daughter in his regard?"

"Yes." Cathbarr fought for self-control, the breast of his mail shirt rising and falling, his bloodshot eyes beginning to circle about the place once more in a helpless and angry wonder.

"O'Donnell Dubh," he went on at last, "Nuala O'Malley sends you this word. Give Brian Buidh over to her, and she will pay you what ransom you demand."

"What alliance is there between Brian and her?" asked O'Donnell softly.

"Brian has given her service, and I have," Cathbarr flung up his head. "Our men lie in Gorumna Castle, there are ships coming from Erris and the isles, and if Brian be slain we shall bear on this hold and give no quarter. We have four hundred men now, and five ships are coming from the North."

The Dark Master gazed quietly at the giant, Vere taking no part in the talk. But Brian, watching also, saw that which brought a mocking smile to O'Donnell's pallid face. Cathbarr had no fear of any man, and lies did not come easily to his lips; when he spoke of the force lying in Gorumna, and of help from Erris, his face gave him away. Brian saw Turlough behind that tale, but Cathbarr was no man to carry it off with success.

"Well," laughed the Dark Master, "none the less shall Brian be slain. Carry back that word to Nuala O'Malley."

Cathbarr's mighty chest heaved like a barrel near to bursting. Brian was minded to break his promise, but Murrough's pistol was at his head, and he could but lie quietly and watch. The giant's face flushed somewhat.

"I have not finished," said he. "My business for the Bird Daughter is done in truth, but now I have to speak a word of my own."

"Let us hear it," returned O'Donnell.

"It is this." Cathbarr drew himself up. "I am more your enemy than is Brian. Let him go, O'Donnell Dubh, and take me in his place, for I love him."

A sudden amazed silence fell on every man there, and but for Murrough's warning hand Brian would have sat up. O'Donnell's jaw fell for an instant, then his head drew in between his shoulders, he put a hand to Vere's arm, and whispered something. The royalist nodded, a grin on his coarse face, and the Dark Master settled back easily. Cathbarr still stood waiting, the ax held out before him, and a glory in his wide eyes.

"I would sooner hold you than Brian," and O'Donnell spoke softly. "If you will to take his place and die in his stead, Cathbarr, then loose that ax of yours."

Brian saw that Cathbarr was lost indeed, for the Dark Master was not likely to give over his pact with the royalists so easily. Cathbarr heaved up his ax with a great laugh, like a child; he brought it down on the stones, but if he had meant to break it the effort was vain. The huge weapon clanged down and bounded high out of his two hands, so that men drew back in awe; but the ax whirled twice in the cresset-light, then fell and slithered over the flagging beneath a table, and no man touched it.

"Take me," said Cathbarr simply.

"Nay," answered the Dark Master calmly, though his eyes flamed, "kneel down."

Cathbarr stood breathing heavily for an instant, then slowly obeyed. Brian saw that his curly beard was beginning to stand out from his face, but no word came from him as he went to his knees.

"Now," went on the Dark Master, "pray me for Brian's life, mighty one."

The giant struggled with himself, for humiliation came hard to him. Then his voice fell curiously low, terrible in its self-restraint.

"I pray you for the life of Yellow Brian, O'Donnell."

Brian forced himself up, thinking to cry out a warning before it was too late; but Murrough's hand closed over his mouth and forced him back relentlessly.

"Bring ropes," said the Dark Master, and ordered Cathbarr to his feet.

Men hastened out, and returned with a length of rope, binding the giant's arms behind his back, from elbow to wrist. Then the Dark Master laughed harshly, but Vere leaned toward him, his face troubled.

"Do not carry this thing farther, O'Donnell," said the royalist hoarsely. "This man is a fool, but he has a great heart. Let be."

For answer the Dark Master whirled on him with such fury in his snarl that Vere drew back hastily, and no more words passed between them at that time. O'Donnell rose and walked down the hall toward Cathbarr, in his hand a little switch that he used upon that wolfhound of his.

"Now," he said softly, yet his voice pierced hard through the dead stillness, "in token that your humility in this affair is without guile, Cathbarr of the Ax, bow your head to me."

The giant obeyed, closing his eyes. The Dark Master lifted his hand and cut him twice across the head with his switch, while Brian gasped in amazement and looked for Cathbarr to strike out with his foot. But although the giant shuddered, he made no move, and the Dark Master strode back to his seat with a laugh. Then Cathbarr raised his face, and Brian saw that it was terribly convulsed.

"Do with me as you wish," he said, still in that low voice. "But now let Brian be freed in my presence."

The Dark Master flung back his head in a laugh, and when the men saw his jest, a great howl of derision rang up to the rafters. Only Vere's officers looked on with black faces, for it was plain that this affair was none of their liking. A look of simple wonder came into Cathbarr's wide-set eyes.

"Why do you not loose him?" he asked quietly.

"Fetch the man out, Murrough," ordered the Dark Master. "Shoot him if he speaks."

Now, whether through some shred of mercy—for he knew well that Brian would cry out—or for some other reason, Murrough leaned down swiftly to Brian's ear.

"Careful," he whispered as he motioned his men forward. "Play the part, and mind that this thing is not yet finished."

The warning came in good time, and cooled Brian's raging impulse. He was lifted from behind the table, his chains clanking, and laid upon it; Cathbarr gave a great start and bellowed out one furious word:

"Dead!"

"Nay," smiled the Dark Master. "His eyes are open, and he is but weak with his wounds, Cathbarr. Now say—would you sooner that we cut off that right hand of his, or blinded him? One of these things I shall do before I loose him, for I said only that I would take your life for his."

Brian saw that the Dark Master was only playing with the giant, for well he knew that Vere wanted to take him back to Galway whole and sound. But Cathbarr knew nothing of this, and as the whole terrible trickery flashed over his simple mind he lifted a face that was dark with blood and passion.

"Do not play with me!" he cried out, his voice deep and angry. "Loose him!"

Then O'Donnell leaned back in his chair, laughing with his men, and waved a careless hand toward Vere.

"He is not mine," he grinned. "I have given him to the royalists, for hanging at Galway. You, however, are now mine to slay."

Whether the Dark Master indeed meant to break his plighted faith, Brian never knew. Cathbarr took a single step forward, his curly beard writhing and standing out, and his whole face so terrible to look on that all laughter was stricken dead in the hall.

"You lied to me!" he cried hoarsely. "You lied to me!"

O'Donnell laughed.

"Aye, Cathbarr. Your master goes back to Galway to be hung—he is out of my hands, but you are in them. However, since I have passed my word on your safe-conduct, I think that I may hold to it."

But the giant had not heard him. Throwing back his head, he gave one deep groan of anguish, and his shoulders began to move very slowly as his chest heaved up. All the while his eyes were fixed on the Dark Master, while the whole hall watched him in awe; not even Brian or O'Donnell himself guessed what that slow movement of Cathbarr's body boded.

"Best put chains upon him, Murrough," said the Dark Master, his teeth shining under his drooping mustache.

Vere cried out in sudden wonder.

" 'Fore Gad! Look!"

Then indeed the Dark Master looked, and sprang to his feet, and one great shout of alarm and fear shrilled up from those watching. For as Cathbarr stood there, the veins had suddenly come out on his face and neck, and with a dull sound the ropes had broken on his arms, and he was free.

Murrough rushed forward, and his pistol spat fire. Cathbarr, with his eyes still on the Dark Master, put out a hand and Murrough went whirling away with a dull groan. Then the giant rushed.

O'Donnell did not stay for that meeting, but slipped away like a shadow into his surging men, yelling at them to fire. There were few muskets in the hall, however, and an instant later Cathbarr had reached the table where Vere still sat astounded. He brought down a fist on the royalist's steel cap, and Vere coughed horribly and fell out of his chair with his skull crushed.

Now a musket roared out, and another. But Cathbarr caught up the oaken table and faced around on the men who were surging forward at him; lifting the ten-foot table as though it were paper, he bellowed something and rushed at them, casting the table in a great heave. It fell squarely on the front rank, and then indeed fear came upon the hall. For Cathbarr's foot had struck against his ax, and he rose with it in his hand.

There was a din of screams and shouts, for half the men were struggling to get out of the hall and the rest were rushing to get at Cathbarr. Another musket crashed, and in the smoke Brian saw the giant stagger, recover, and go bellowing into the crowd.

Brian struggled from the table, groaned with pain, and then stood watching. He could walk, but his weakness and the chains on his wrists and ankles hindered him from being of any advantage to Cathbarr, though he lifted his voice in a shout of encouragement.

Cathbarr heard the shout, and roared out with delight. A musket-ball had cut across his forehead, and with the blood dripping from his beard he looked more like a demon than a man. The huge ax flashed in the smoky light, and before it men groaned and shrieked and gave back; it cleaved steel and flesh, or smashed helms and heads together, and the Dark Master had slipped from the place, so that his men had no leader.

Over the roar of fear-mad men, over the storm of shrieks and shouts, over the dust and smoke, rose the mighty bellow of Cathbarr and the thudding blows of his ax. The royalist officers were fighting around the doorway, while O'Donnell's men were trying to make head against the giant, but he swept through them like a whirlwind, awing them more by his ferocious aspect and his mad rage than by the half-seen effect of his terrific strength.

Little by little they eddied out from the door. Men lay all about, tables were overturned, and through the crowd swirled the terrible ax, leaving a path of dead in its wake. Brian staggered to the motionless form of Colonel Vere, and reaching down drew a pistol from the dead man's belt. His strength was flooding back to him, and in spite of the agony caused by every movement, he clanked slowly down toward the door. At sight of his chained and bandage-swathed figure a wild shriek welled up, and when he laughed and fired into the midst of them all opposition ceased.

Cathbarr still sought the Dark Master, raging back and forth, smiting and smiting with never a pause in the flaillike sweep of his long arms. He saw Brian standing there, and emitted a wild bellow of joy, but never ceased from his smiting. Out through the door poured a stream of maddened figures, for blind panic had come on every man there, and Cathbarr's was not the only weapon that drew blood as the men fought for exit.

Brian laughed again, for now he knew that he would die in no long time, but it would not be under the torturers. Cathbarr cleared the hall, sent the last man flying out with an arm lopped from him, and swung to the huge doors after kicking two or three bodies from his way. When the beam had dropped into place and they were alone with the dead and dying, he turned to Brian and flung out his arms.

"Careful!" exclaimed Brian, seizing his hand. "None of your bear-hugs, old friend," and he swiftly told of his tortures. Tears ran down the giant's blood-strewn face as he listened, and with the tenderness of a woman he picked up Brian and carried him back to a table, setting him on it.

"First for these chains, brother," he cried, going back for his ax. "We may yet win out against these devils."

"Small chance," smiled Brian grimly. "I cannot swing a blade, and we cannot hold this hall for long. Besides, you have some wounds."

Cathbarr roared out a laugh, exuberantly as a boy, and carefully spread Brian's legs open on the table.

"Hold quiet!" he cautioned, and swung up the ax. Down it flashed, the thinner blade sheared through the chain an inch from Brian's ankle and split the oak beneath, and Cathbarr drew back for a second blow.

Four times he struck, and the blows smote off the chains from each wrist and ankle, although the locked rings still remained. But Brian was free, and when he gained his feet he found the exercise had somewhat loosened his muscles, and he picked up a sword.

"We can at least die fighting, Cathbarr," he said, and looked into the giant's eyes. "And, brother, I thank you."

"Nonsense!" blurted out Cathbarr, wiping the blood from his eyes and grinning through his beard. "Turlough Wolf has our men hidden around this royalist camp, and the Bird Daughter has a boat outside the castle. We cannot get through the royalists, but there is a chance that we can get to the shore. Besides, she has ships and men coming from her kinsmen in the North. Now, how shall we get away?"

Brian shook his head. "I can hardly walk, Cathbarr, to say nothing of swimming or fighting. There is a rear door out of the hall, yonder, but no use trying it."

"Perchance I have still some strength," grinned Cathbarr, picking up his ax. "Let us have a look at that rear door, before they come at us with muskets."

CHAPTER XII

HOW THE DARK MASTER
WAS RUINED

THE FEAR that had come upon the O'Donnells was so great that not until pikemen entered the castle from the camp could the Dark Master get men at the doors of the hall. And this proved the salvation of Brian and Cathbarr, for when they left the hall by the rear door and slipped through the corridors, they came out upon the rear or seaward battlements of the castle.

These they found denuded of men, while from the courtyard and front of the keep were rising shouts and batterings, whereat Cathbarr chuckled.

"They are all drawn around to the front, brother. Now, how to get down from here?"

Brian looked around in the starlight, but saw that there was no gate or other opening in the walls. He began to lose hope again; once the Dark Master had burst into the great hall he would scatter men over the whole castle, and their shrift would be short. At this point the walls were some thirty feet high, and pointing out to the sea stood four of the bastards, with balls piled beside them.

"Now if we had a rope," he said, "the matter would not be hard. Is that boat near the shore?"

"Not so far that I cannot make them hear," grinned Cathbarr, opening his mouth to shout, but Brian stopped him.

"Be careful—do you want to draw down the O'Donnells

likewise? Now, cut the ropes from these cannon, and if we have time we shall yet get down safe."

Cathbarr rushed off in delight, and began hewing at the recoil-ropes which bound the bastards and their carriages to their places. Brian followed him, seizing the ropes and trying to knot the strands hastily and with no little pain to himself; but now the hope of escape began to thrill through him, and for the first time since sighting the Dark Master's stronghold he began to think that he might yet get away. However, he could do little knotting with one hand, and not until Cathbarr impatiently took over the task was it finished. At the same instant a great burst of yells rose over the castle.

"Hasten!" cried Brian, as the other began fastening the line to a cannon. "I can use one hand—"

"Save your strength," grunted Cathbarr, lifting him after swinging the loop of his ax around his neck. "Catch me about the neck with your good arm, and trust me for the rest, brother."

Brian did as he was ordered, since there was no time for lowering him down. The giant scrambled over the edge, gripping the twisting rope, and Brian tightened his lips to keep down his groans, for the agony was cruel to him. He was forced against the body of Cathbarr, and swirl after swirl of pain went over him at each touch on his burns.

The giant grunted once or twice, for he had many slight wounds also, but with the rope gripped in hands and feet, he lowered away steadily. At length they reached the ground, and the scattered rocks along the shore were but a few yards away.

Cathbarr sent his bull-like voice roaring out at the stars, while Brian clung weakly to him and searched the waters. He could see nothing, but suddenly there drifted in a faint shout, and Cathbarr bellowed once more.

"Swim for it," said Brian, as torches began to move along the walls above. "If those cannon are not loaded, we're safe."

Cathbarr nodded, and caught up the body of Brian tenderly enough in one arm, as he splashed out. The icy water shocked

Brian's brain awake and drove the pain out of him momentarily, and before Cathbarr was waist-deep he heard a hail and saw the dark shape of a galley approaching.

Muskets flashed out from the walls, and their bullets whistled overhead, but five minutes later Brian was on the galley, Cathbarr was clambering over the side, and the light boat was being rowed out again.

Brian thought his senses were slipping away when he found Nuala O'Malley herself holding his head as he lay in the stern, while men flung cloaks around him; but warm tears dripped on his face, and she patted his arm soothingly.

"Lie quiet," she said, but Brian would not, for already his brain was leaping ahead, and he knew that there was work to be done.

"Tell me," he asked eagerly, "are my men camped around the royalists? Is help indeed coming to you from the North?"

"Yes," she replied, trying to quiet him. "A pigeon came in from Erris to-day, with word that two ships with men were on the way to help me. When I returned from the South and found that the plague had been at Gorumna, I sent off asking for help, and now it is coming."

"Then send word to Turlough!" cried Brian eagerly. "Tell him to throw my men on the royalist camp *to-night* and drive the pikemen into the castle! Colonel Vere is dead, and there is such confusion that all will think we have more than two hundred men. If we can leaguer them there until your ships come, we may win all at a blow!"

Nuala found instantly that there was meat in the plan, and as they were rowing out to meet one of her caracks, promised to send in the galley with word to Turlough when they got aboard the larger ship.

This they were no great while in doing. Brian knew nothing of it, for upon the Bird Daughter's word he had dropped away into a faint once more. With this Nuala O'Malley was quite content, so that when Brian wakened he was greatly refreshed and found himself lying bandaged on a bunk with the sunlight coming through a stern-port beside him, and the Bird Daughter watching him with food and drink ready.

"Take of this first," she smiled; "then we will talk."

Brian obeyed, being very thirsty and ravenously hungered. He had little pain except when he tried to move, and so he ate as he lay, propped up with folded garments, and watched the Bird Daughter. She refused to speak until he had eaten the meat and cakes she had fetched, but when he smiled and asked for a razor her grave face rippled with frank laughter, and her deep violet eyes danced as they looked into his.

"I am sorry I have none," she said mockingly. "So you must wait till we come to port again. Just at present we are off Slyne Head and bearing northward."

"What!" Brian stared at her. "Are you in jest?"

It appeared that she was not, for she was sailing north to meet those ships of her kinsmen, and to hasten them back with her. Meantime Cathbarr had been sent ashore to meet Turlough and hold the Dark Master and his royalists in check. Nuala had sent fifty of her men to join Turlough, left twenty to hold her castle, and had ten with her upon the carack. It seemed likely that Turlough and Cathbarr could hold the Dark Master penned up for a few days at least, even with fewer men; if they could not, said Nuala shortly, they had best sit at spinning-wheels for the rest of their lives.

"You are a wonderful girl!" said Brian, and fell asleep again.

He remembered little of that voyage, for they met two caracks crowded with men off Innishark that afternoon, found they were the expected O'Malleys from the North, and turned back with them at once. Brian wakened again that same evening, but Nuala refused to let him go on deck until the following morning, when they sighted Bertraghboy Bay. Then Brian discarded most of his bandages, dressed, and, with his left arm in a sling, joined the Bird Daughter on the quarterdeck. He found that his burns were well on toward healing, for he could walk slowly without great pain, and had every confidence that he could sit a horse if need be.

Sailing past Bertragh Castle, the three ships went on up the bay and cast anchor. It was not hard to see that Turlough and Cathbarr had done their work well, for in passing the castle they had made out that the royalist pikemen had been driven inside, and there was some musketry to be heard at times. No sooner had the anchor-cables roared out, indeed, than a band of men came riding toward the shore, and Nuala sent off a boat for them. She had known nothing of Cathbarr's deeds at the castle until Brian had told her of them, and on seeing that the giant was among those coming off, she smiled at Brian.

"Now you shall see how a girl can conquer a giant, Yellow Brian!"

Brian laughed and waved a hand to Turlough, who was beside Cathbarr in the boat. As the men came over the rail, Nuala quietly pushed him aside and faced the giant, sharply bidding him kneel. Cathbarr had been all for rushing forward to Brian, and obeyed with an ill grace, when Nuala quickly leaned forward and kissed him on the brow.

"That is for bravery and faith," she said. "Truly, I would that you served me!"

Poor Cathbarr grew redder than the Bird Daughter's cloak. He started to his feet, gazed around sheepishly, found all men laughing at him—and did the best thing he could have done, which was to go to his knees again and put Nuala's hand to his lips.

"While my master serves you, I serve you," he blurted out, and this answer must have pleased Nuala mightily, for she flushed, laughed, and bade all down into the cabin.

Brian greeted Turlough with no little joy, but beyond assurances that all went well, gained no knowledge of what had happened. Nuala had sent for the O'Malley chieftains, and proposed to hold a conference at once.

The O'Malleys arrived from the other ships in a scant five

minutes—dark, silent men who spoke little, but spoke to the point. Art Bocagh, or the Lame, had had one leg hamstrung in his youth, but Brian took him for a dangerous man in battle; while his cousin Shaun the Little was a very short man with tremendous shoulders.

Nuala took her seat at the head of the stern-cabin table, and the position of affairs was gone over carefully.

It seemed that no sooner had Turlough learned from Cathbarr of what had taken place in the castle, and that Brian was safe on shipboard, than he drove his men down pell-mell on the camp, just before dawn. Any other man would have been exhausted by the events of that night, but Cathbarr had led them in the assault. The result had been that, with hardly any resistance, they had slain some four-score of the pikemen, and would have captured or slain them all had it not been for the Dark Master's cannon which drove them back.

The better part of the royalist officers had fallen, either then or under the ax of Cathbarr in the hall of the castle. In fact, after learning that he had slain some nineteen persons on that occasion, Cathbarr had taken no few airs upon himself. Vanity was to him as natural as to a child, and Brian hugely enjoyed watching the giant strut. However, what remained of Vere's five hundred pikemen were in the castle, joined to the Dark Master's men; and Turlough's advice was that since there must be some seven hundred mouths to feed, the safest plan was to bide close and force the fight to come to them, rather than to take it to O'Donnell.

"There is reason against that, Turlough Wolf," said Brian quickly. "The Dark Master has men on the hills, and if news is borne to Galway of what has happened, we are like to have a larger army on our heels than we can cope with."

"I have attended to O'Donnell's watchers," said Turlough grimly. "When Cathbarr bore word of the pact from Gorumna Castle, I sent out horsemen and we swept the hills bare of men.

O'Donnell has no more than are in the castle, and a score of our own men are on the roads, watching for any ill."

"How many men have we in all?" spoke up Lame Art O'Malley. "In our ships there are sixty men we can spare for land battle."

"That gives us three hundred in all," replied Turlough to Nuala's questioning glance. "If we take a strong position we should sweep most of O'Donnell's men away at the first charge."

"There you are wrong," said Brian, shaking his head. "Those pikemen are bad foes for cavalry, and our two hundred horsemen would shatter on them if they stood firm."

"Not if we choose our ground," said the Bird Daughter, her eyes flashing. "Nay, *I* am master here, my friends! Now this is my rede. We shall not waste men by attacking the castle, unless forced to it by an army from Galway. Instead, we will wait until the Dark Master is driven out by hunger; then we will fall on him and destroy him utterly.

"Yellow Brian, you have some knowledge of war, and you shall take this matter in charge. Cathbarr, do you command fifty horse, with the men from our ships here, and keep the Dark Master in play. With the remainder, we shall wait in whatever spot Brian shall choose, and before many days are sped I think that Bertragh will be mine again."

The Bird Daughter had her way, since none could find much against her plan; and that afternoon Brian went ashore with her and the O'Malleys, leaving the three ships at anchor under a small guard. Turlough had made camp a short mile from the castle, on a little hill among the farms; both Nuala and the O'Malley men were somewhat surprised at finding the O'Donnell women and children safe and untouched in their own steads.

"I saw to that," laughed Turlough, slanting his crafty eyes at Brian. "I had but to threaten them in Brian's name, and the men only were slain."

"I think that you are a hard master," laughed Nuala, but Brian smiled and pointed to his men, who were pouring out to meet him with shouts of joy.

"All men do not rule by fear alone, Bird Daughter," he said quietly. She gave him a quick glance. "I found these men riffraff of the wars, and while they have no such love for me as Cathbarr here, I think they had liefer follow me than any other leader."

After that Nuala said little concerning Brian's discipline.

That night Nuala and Brian took up headquarters at one of the larger farms, and while Cathbarr went before the castle to keep the Dark Master in check and allow none to leave the place, they called in a number of those men O'Donnell had loaned to Brian, and questioned them about the provisioning of the castle.

From these they found that there was good store of all things for the usual garrison, but with seven hundred men to feed the Dark Master would be forced out speedily. So with the dawn Brian and Turlough rode forth to select a battleground, and while Brian was very sore and riding caused him great pain at first, he soon found himself in better shape.

Turlough picked a hollow in the road a mile farther from the castle, flanked on either hand by woods and hillsides where men might lie hidden. Brian found it good, and that afternoon a part of their horsemen were shifted thither in readiness.

For the next three days there was little done. Twice the Dark Master attempted sallies with what few horsemen he had left, but on each occasion Cathbarr's horse smote his men and drove them back. To be sure, O'Donnell thundered with his bastards, but the guns only burned up good powder, for Brian would allow no assault made.

By Turlough's advice, however, they brought about the Dark Master's fall through certain prisoners made in the two sallies.

These captives were led through the depleted central camp, though they knew nothing of that picked place farther back. Having been allowed to see what men Brian had here, Turlough slyly drove Cathbarr into parading his vanity before them; and in all innocence the giant told how he could put the Dark

Master's men to flight single-handed, and of his anxiety lest the O'Donnells should fear to fight in the open. What was more, Brian affected to be utterly shattered by his wounds, and with that the prisoners were sent back with a message offering quarter to all within the castle save the Dark Master himself.

Early the next morning a horseman came riding fast from Cathbarr with word that the garrison was stirring. Without delay, Brian donned a mail-shirt, bound his useless left arm to his side, and mounted. The Bird Daughter insisted on accompanying him, and stilled his dismayed protests by asserting her feudal superiority; in the end she had her way.

Leaving her kinsmen and a hundred more men to dispute O'Donnell's passage and give back slowly before him with Cathbarr, she and Brian rode to their men among the trees on the hillsides over the hollow in the road. Here they had a hundred and fifty men, composed of the Scots troopers and the pick of the others, and Nuala took one side of the road while Brian took the other. Then, being well hidden, they waited.

Brian was savagely determined to slay the Dark Master that day, and came near to doing it. Presently a man galloped up to say that O'Donnell and six hundred men were on the road, having left the rest to hold the castle. A little later Cathbarr's retreating force came in sight, and after them marched O'Donnell. He had deployed his muskets in front and rear, and rode in the midst of his pikemen, whose banner of England blew out bravely in the morning wind.

At the edge of the dip in the road Cathbarr led his men in full flight down the hollow and up the farther rise, where he halted as if to dispute the Dark Master further. There were barely a dozen mounted men with O'Donnell, and he made no pursuit, but marched steadily along with his muskets pecking at Cathbarr's men. When he had come between the wooded hillsides, however, Cathbarr came charging down the road; the pikemen settled their pikes three deep to receive him, and with that Brian led out his men among the trees and swooped down with an ax swinging in his right hand.

Alive to his danger, the Dark Master tried to receive his charge, but at that instant Nuala's men burst down on the other flank. Brian headed his men, and at sight of him a yell of dismay went up from the O'Donnells. A moment later the pikemen's array was broken and the fight disintegrated into a wild affray wherein the horsemen had much the better of it.

Brian tried to cut his way to the Dark Master, but when O'Donnell saw the pikemen shattered he knew that the day was lost. He gathered his dozen horsemen and went at Cathbarr viciously; Brian saw the two meet, saw O'Donnell's blade slip under the ax and Cathbarr go from the saddle, then the Dark Master had broken through the ring and was riding hard for the North.

Brian wheeled his horse instantly, found the Bird Daughter at his side, and with a score of men behind them they rode out of the battle in pursuit. It proved useless, however, for the Dark Master had the better horseflesh; after half an hour he was gaining rapidly, and with a bitter groan Brian drew rein at last.

"No use, Nuala," he said. "I must wait until my strength has come back to me, for I have done too much and can go no farther."

The girl reined in beside him, and her hand went out to his, and he found himself gazing deep into her eyes.

"For what you have done, Brian," she said simply, "thanks. Now let us ride back, for I think there is work before us, and we shall see the Dark Master soon enough."

"I am not minded to wait his coming," quoth Yellow Brian darkly, and they returned.

CHAPTER XIII

BRIAN RIDES TO VENGEANCE

"THEN YOU are intent on this vengeance, master?" asked Turlough thoughtfully.

"Yes," answered Brian. "I here take oath that I will never cut hair nor beard again until I have seen the Dark Master dead."

"You are not like to have a chance at your hair very soon," laughed out Lame Art O'Malley. "But that is a good oath, Yellow Brian."

"Then I think this is a better plan," spoke up Turlough Wolf. "Give me ten men, Brian, and I will go to Galway. I will soon get traces of O'Donnell; and if he goes into the north to get men of his own sept" (tribe or family), "as I think most likely, I will send back word, and we can follow him."

"Do it," said Brian, and Turlough was gone that night.

This discussion took place in the hollow, where the fight was soon over after the flight of the Dark Master. Out of the six hundred who had left the castle, two hundred had been O'Donnell's men. Half of these remained and took service with Brian at once. Of the four hundred pikemen, three hundred had gone down fighting like the stubborn south-country men they were, and the rest took service with Nuala O'Malley. They were most of them Kerry men, and well disposed toward ships and piracy.

Brian had lost in all fifty men in that battle, while the Dark Master had given Cathbarr a goodly thrust through the shoulder, which had let out most of the giant's vanity and promised to give the huge ax some time to rest and rust. So, then, Brian found himself heading two hundred and fifty men of his own, with Nuala's hundred O'Malleys, when they rode down again to Bertragh Castle.

This had been left in charge of a hundred men under Red Murrough, who had not been slain, but only wounded by Cathbarr's fist, that night in the great hall. Having left a party to bring in the wounded in wagons from the farms, they arrived before the castle shortly after noon. Cathbarr was left in charge of the camp, and Brian rode up to the gates with Nuala and her two kinsmen, with a flag of truce.

Murrough and his men were put into consternation by the news Brian gave them. After much stroking of his matted beard, Murrough proposed to surrender the castle on condition that he hold his post of lieutenant. Brian laughed, for he had other views on the subject.

"You sold your master, and you will have no chance to sell me, Murrough. I will give you the ten pounds I owe you and a good horse. Refuse, and I slay you when we storm the castle."

The end of that matter was that Murrough assented. An hour later he opened the gates, his men taking service with the rest under Brian. Then, having obtained his ten English pounds and a horse, he waved farewell to his men and rode away; and what became of him after that is not set forth in the chronicle, so he comes no more into this tale.

Nuala loaded her fifty men into her carack, and sent them home that night to Gorumna in case of need, proposing to follow later with Lame Art, Shaun the Little, and her Kerry recruits. The O'Malley cousins intended going south, since their affair had been so unexpectedly ended, and picking up a Spanish ship or two before returning home.

"And now, what of your plans?" asked Nuala, as she and Brian sat together that night before the huge fireplace in the hall, where Brian had been burned and where Cathbarr had fought so well. "Of course, we can settle rents later on."

"When there are farms to gather rents from," laughed Brian, stretching out easily. He lifted his bandaged left hand, gazing at it. "First, I am minded to rest here and wait for news from Galway. The bones in this hand of mine are not broken, from what I can make out, and it will soon knit. As soon as may be, I shall ride after the Dark Master; when I have paid my debts, I will then be in shape to look for a castle for myself."

"Then you are determined to kill O'Donnell?" and she looked at him sidewise.

"He has my Spanish blade," said Brian. "It is good Toledo steel, and I want it back again."

"You have three hundred and fifty men here," she observed. "Can you feed them?"

"You have food in Gorumna—send me some. When I am well again I shall ride with most of them, which will lessen the burden. With the spring I will take lands between here and Slyne Head, for now I am strong enough to defend what I take."

"I shall also send you some of my pigeons, Brian. They are born and bred on Gorumna Isle, and if you tie a message to them they will—"

"I know," nodded Brian. "I have seen them used in Spain."

With that she described how she used these pigeons, and Brian saw that it was not by strength alone that this girl had maintained her position. She kept men in Galway, Kinvarra, and elsewhere, as far south as the Shannon and as far north as Erris, with others at Limerick and Tuam and Castlebar. In this wise she got news of what was passing in Connaught and Munster before most men had it, and more than one foreign ship had found her caracks waiting for it through the same means, since she held a privateer commission given her by Blake to legalize her sea-roving. Also, she had pigeons which carried return messages, chiefly to her kinsmen in Erris.

"And what is your goal, Bird Daughter?" Brian turned to her, his blue eyes clinching on her violet ones. "What will the end of all this wild life of yours be?"

"I do not know," she answered him, and turned away from his eyes to stare down into the fire. "In the end I may be forced into marriage, though I think not, for I have some will of my own in that regard." She laughed out suddenly and looked up. "Two years ago Stephen Lynch sent me a fair screed in all the glory of his chevron and three shamrocks and wolf crest, saying that he was coming in one of his ships to marry me."

"And did he ever come?" smiled Brian.

"Yes; but I took his ship from him and sent him home again by road, tied to a horse," she rippled out merrily. "Poor Stephen! The Bodkins never let the Lynches hear the last of it until Stephen fell fighting against Coote, and there was an end of it and him, too. When are you going to tell me your name, Brian?"

At the sudden question Brian was tempted, but forbore.

"When I have slain the Dark Master," he laughed.

"Then you are likely to be bearded worse than Cathbarr," she mocked him gaily. "Unless, indeed, you break that oath you swore this morning."

"Not I," returned Brian shortly. "I am not given to light oaths or light pacts, Bird Daughter. I think I shall get me a ship and go cruising some day."

"Come with me," she said, rising, "and you may win food and wine without begging from your overlord. Well, now for that chamber Cathbarr fixed up for me. *Beannacht leath!*"

Somewhat to his surprise, the next morning Brian found that Nuala was extremely businesslike and even curt. Knowing little of women, he tried to find wherein he had offended; failed utterly, and gave over the attempt on seeing that Nuala preferred the company of Cathbarr.

Then, remembering that kiss she had given the giant aboard ship, he concluded that the Bird Daughter was drawn by the physical magnificence of the man, which gave him a little bitterness. So he merely set his jaw the harder and said nothing of the thing that lay in his heart to any one. For that matter, he was not quite sure himself what the thing was; but he knew that he had never seen a woman such as the Bird Daughter in all his life, and was not apt to find another.

Turlough having departed on his mission, Brian fell back on Cathbarr to act as lieutenant; with Nuala herself, the work of getting the castle in shape proceeded apace. The Bertragh hold was built on a cliff that rose from the plain on the one hand, and sloped down to the water on the other; had the Dark Master not fallen into Turlough's trap, he might have turned out the pikemen to shift for themselves and have held the castle with his own men for as long as he wished.

Indeed, Brian found that the removal of danger and the taking of the castle had somewhat puffed up his men, lessening their fear of him. So, on the second day, he quelled a free fight that rose among them, hanged ten of the worst, and after this the others became as lambs before him.

Upon exploring the castle, Brian was delighted to find it well equipped in all things except prisoners. The Dark Master had had little use for captives, it seemed, and his dungeons were in sad disrepair. However, there was good store of powder, provisions in moderation, a well within the castle, and no lack of arms and munitions of war. Brian promptly took the chamber of O'Donnell for his own use—a large tower-room well furnished in English style, and having the luxury of a fireplace besides.

The construction of the building was simple—a large stone structure with embattled walls, running down close to the sea behind and rising above the plain in front. Save for the courtyard, the walls were not separated from the building proper, and there was one high tower, on which the flagstaff had been shattered since O'Donnell had taken the place, for he was not given to flags and display. Besides a dozen of the large bastards, there were five falcons, with plenty of ball.

Therefore, Brian had good reason to be satisfied with his new home. The only thing that rankled was that he held it not for himself, but for the Bird Daughter; and he was determined that when he had settled scores with the Dark Master he would only remain here until he had secured a hold for himself, free of all service.

But settling with O'Donnell Dubh was the first duty he had. Brian recalled his torture and the agony of Cathbarr every time he entered the hall. The iron rings that had been in the floor he had already torn out, while Nuala had taken for her own the lonely wolfhound, which had been left behind by the Dark Master. But Brian, who put all his desire for vengeance in the wish to "get back his Spanish blade," could hardly turn around without having some phase of his sufferings brought back to him.

The men who had been thrown out along the roads had fetched in word that the Dark Master had ridden for Galway, so Brian had great hopes that Turlough would bring back some definite news. If O'Donnell settled in the city, he was determined to go in at all risks and seek out his enemy face to face; the O'Malleys were on good terms with the Bodkins, who in old Galway played *Capulet* to the *Montague* of the Lynch family, and he would be able to command some help in that quarter.

On the fifth day after the castle had been taken, a galley came over from Gorumna Castle bearing news. Cromwell had failed before Duncannon, and promised to fail again at Waterford, and hope was rising high among the royalists, while O'Neill's Ulster army was biding its time in the north until a new leader was chosen by the Confederacy to make head with Ormond against the Parliament armies.

Upon this the O'Malley rovers were impatient to revictual at Gorumna and be off to the south after plunder, so Nuala decided to leave Bertragh the next morning. That night, after Cathbarr had drunk himself asleep and the O'Malleys had sought their ships, the Bird Daughter unexpectedly became very cordial toward Brian once more, and they sat up late before the fireplace.

Brian did not understand it, but he was quite willing to accept it, and when the talk turned on personal matters he was careful to ask no questions concerning Nuala's plans for the future.

Instead, he told her tales of his life at the Spanish court, which interested her vastly, until in the end she broke forth with a passionate outburst.

"Oh, I wish I were a man!" she cried softly and eagerly, looking into the red embers. "All my life I have been among men, and yet not of them; I have had to do with guns and ships and powder, and I think I have not done so ill, yet I have had dreams of other things—things which I hardly know myself."

Astonished though he was at her sudden unfolding of herself, Brian looked at her gravely, his blue eyes very soft as he pierced to her thought.

"Yes," he said gently, "you are a woman, Bird Daughter—and if you were a man I think that you might have gain, but others would have great loss."

"Eh?" She looked straightly at him, unfearing his half-expressed thought. "I do not seek idle compliments, Yellow Brian, from those who serve me."

Brian flushed a little.

"It is hard to receive compliments gracefully," he said, and at that she also colored, but laughed, her eyes still on his.

"There, give grace to my rude tongue, Brian! Of course you meant it—but why?"

"Because there is no woman like you, Nuala—so able to weld men into union, so vibrant with inner power, and yet so womanly withal. It is no little honor to have known you, to have—"

"I wish you would tell me your name, Yellow Brian!"

There was woman's cunning in the placing of that answer, and it took Brian all aback. For a moment he was near to blurting out his whole story; then he took shame for letting a girl's face so run away with him. None the less, he knew well that it was her heart as well as her face, and her spirit as well as her heart, that had captured him; yet, because he had had no dealings with women since leaving Spain some months before, he told himself that if the Bird Daughter had other women near by to compare herself with, less attraction might be found in her.

But he did not pause long upon that thought, sweeping his blue eyes to hers in a smile.

"If you had been a man, Nuala, you had never had fealty from me."

"So—then it *was* pity?" and swift anger leaped into her face.

"Was it pity that drove Cathbarr to proffer his life for mine?" parried Brian, his eyes grave. He felt a great impulse to speak out all that was in him, but crushed it down. Her eyes met his, and held there for a long moment. Then she spoke very calmly:

"When will you take that cruise with me, Yellow Brian?"

"When I have won my Spanish blade again," he smiled, and after that they talked no more of intimate things, yet Brian's heart was glad within him.

With the next morning the Bird Daughter said farewell and went aboard Lame Art's carack. Sorry was Brian to see her go, for he had come to count much on her fine backing and inspiring courage, and knew not if he would ever see her again. As the ships raised anchor, Cathbarr suddenly let off the bastards with a great roar and raised on the shattered flag-pole an ensign he had secretly obtained from Shaun the Little. The ship-cannon barked out in brave answer and hoisted ensigns likewise; but as Brian looked up at the flag overhead, his despondent mood was not heartened. The three-masted ship of the O'Malleys flew above him, where he had much rather flown the red hand of his own house.

"When I have slain the Dark Master," he thought, watching from those same sea-facing battlements where he and Cathbarr had descended, as the two caracks leaped off to the south, "and when I have established myself in some hold, be it never so small, then I shall take back my name again and let the red hand hold what it has gripped. But not until these things have been done, for Brian O'Neill will give fealty to none—no, not even to the Bird Daughter herself."

Thus he thought in his proud bitterness, reckoning not on

what the future was to bring forth. However, he had lost his idea that Nuala might love Cathbarr, and had great gladness of it.

Now there was work to be done, and Brian soon found himself too busy to bother his mind with thoughts of bitterness. Cathbarr had done no little drinking, so that his wound was turning bad, and in no little alarm Brian banished all liquors from him and tended him carefully. Taking a lesson from Red Murrough, he washed out the wound with vinegar, and found that this had its effect.

Since Brian was irked at having to rely on others for his supplies, he rode to all the outlying farms and sent off the families there under escort, with sufficient money to keep them and take them to their homes in the north. Many of them chose to remain, and certain of his men knew of women-folk they wished to bring hither, so that Brian saw he would not lack for farmers and settlers. Enough fodder was obtained to keep his horses for a time; but as this did not satisfy him, he set forth after four days on a cattle-raid to the northeast, riding past the Manturks toward Ashford with ninety men.

He was gone on that raid five days; found to his great joy that his strength had returned to him, and also found a small party of Royalist horse near Lough Corrib. These had been buying up cattle for the Galway garrison, and had collected fifty head; but on Brian's approach they did not stay for dispute, but fled.

So Brian cheerfully sent the fifty head of cattle home with as many men, and with the others swept around through the mountains. With him were two of Cathbarr's axmen, and they led him to the hold occupied by Murrough O'Flaherty of the Kine, where Brian stayed half a day. He concluded a friendship with the mountaineers, promising them powder in exchange for cattle, and they promised, in turn, that within three weeks they would fetch a hundred kine down to Castle Bertragh.

Having thus assured himself of both food and stock for his farms, he rode home again, to find great news awaiting him.

First, there had come a galley from Gorumna with wine and

stores. Nuala sent word that her men in Galway had informed her the Dark Master was there, but in no high favor with Lord Burke and the other commanders. Second, one of Turlough Wolf's men had come in with news which had caused Cathbarr to have the men in all readiness against Brian's return.

The Dark Master was indeed in Galway town, and had made small head with his suit for men, having related that Vere and his pikemen were lost. However, he had been promised some help, provided he could gather any force of his own and would hold Bertragh for the Royalists. Cromwell had been driven back at Waterford, but Cork had risen for him, and his men had entered there.

So the Dark Master was going to the north to get him men in Sligo, as Turlough had predicted he would do, and his plan was to raise a force, bring down those Donegal pirates with whom he was in alliance, and set on Bertragh by sea and land, as Brian himself had aimed at doing. Turlough said that he was following, but would leave men at Swineford and Tobercurry with further news of what happed.

"Good!" cried Brian joyfully. "Cathbarr, have a hundred and fifty men saddled at dawn—what is this?"

Turlough's messenger handed him a paper. It was a safe-conduct issued by the Confederacy and Royalist leaders in the name of one Stephen Burke, and where the wily Wolf had gotten it the messenger did not know. But it might come in useful, since there were few parliament men in Sligo and Mayo, and Brian tucked it away with a laugh.

"Then to the north at dawn—and O'Donnell shall not escape me this time!"

CHAPTER XIV

HOW THE STORM FARED NORTH

NOW, IT was no easy matter for a band of horsemen to ride from Galway to Sligo in that day, unless they were known men and rode for the king or the Confederacy. Scattered bands of men had come into the west from Ulster and Leinster, and these had driven out what Parliament men had landed; through the early years of the war Owen Ruadh's men had swept all the west country, and now the land was resting, waiting for the storm that was fated to come upon it when the rest of Ireland had been crushed under the heel of Ireton. Enniskillen alone, in Fermanagh, held out for Parliament.

So, while the larger towns were all under Irish authority, the hill-country was full of seething parties from all armies, most of them being ravagers and outlaws who would fear to lay hand on so large a party as Brian's. But little Brian cared for them, and without let or pause he drove north to Ashford and so into the lowlands.

Knowing that he must return again by the same way, he avoided the larger towns and pushed hard for Swineford, where he would find word from Turlough. More than once he met parties of men on the road, but these were not anxious to question him, and it was not until he was riding around Claremorris that men began to feel his heavy hand.

With Lough Garra falling behind on the left, and Claremorris at safe distance on the right, Brian was clattering along on the third morning. His men carried muskets slung at their saddles, with bandoliers of cartridges at their waists ready for quick action; and well it was that they were so prepared. Searching ahead with narrowed eyes, Brian caught a quick glint of steel on the road, and in no long time he made out a party of a hundred men riding toward him. Brian got ready both his ax and his safe-conduct, and rode forward without pause.

Now, he had brought with him most of those Scots troopers he had taken into service, and as the other party drew near he heard a swift yell of "Albanach!" that boded no good. But Brian shouted to them and asked who they were.

"None of your affair!" answered their leader, a huge, dark man. "Who are you?"

"Stephen Burke from Galway," answered Brian; but before the words left him he saw a musket flash, and one of his men fell.

Upon that, no more words were wasted. Brian threw up his ax and dug in his spurs, with his men behind; and when they loosed their muskets they rode on the hundred with butts swinging. This was a new kind of warfare in Connaught, and before Brian's ax had struck twice the field was won. From two prisoners he found that the band was composed of a levy of the O'Connors out of the Storm Mountains.

"That is not well for our return," said one of his lieutenants. "We will have the whole country up after this battle, and we have lost ten men."

"Then we shall have the more need of recruits," quoth Brian, and let his prisoners go free, since they would take no service, but only cursed him.

However, Brian was not ill pleased, since he found that he was nearly sped of his wounds, though his left hand gave him some trouble at times. His pleasure was speedily cured, for when they camped that night on the hither side of Kiltarnagh there came a rush of men toward dawn, and before they were beaten off twenty of Brian's men were dead. Five prisoners were taken, and when two of these had been hung, the other three confessed that the attack had been made by certain O'Connors from the southern end of Lough Conn, to whose villages fugitives had come from the affray of the previous morning.

With that, Brian took counsel with some of his men who knew the country, and it was their advice that he give up the ride and return home.

"I will not," said Brian shortly. "This war was not of my seeking, but thirty of my men have been slain. Guide me to these villages, and I will take blood-fine."

This he did because he needs must. His men did no ravaging, and were in need of provisions, while he was minded to fill up his ranks. Also, by taking sharp vengeance, he knew that on his return he was not like to be molested.

So he turned aside and rode fast for Lough Conn, which he reached the next evening, and there came a storm of men on all that country. Twice through the days that followed Brian had to fight hard—once against a muster of the O'Connors, and once against a large force of ravaging hillsmen under one Fitzgerald. Him Brian slew with a blow of his ax that went from shoulder to saddle.

From his men he gained fifty recruits and no small booty, both of money and horses; and from the O'Connors he took bitter blood-fine for his slain men in spare horses and provisions.

These doings are set down briefly in the chronicle; but when Brian turned east again, with Swineford a hard day's ride away, he once more had a hundred and fifty men at his back, with a good store of all things, while his name was one that spread fear. He left his men camped two miles out of Swineford, on the Moy, and rode next morning into the town with a dozen horsemen only.

In the town was quartered a small force of Maguires from Fermanagh, and as he rode in Brian was halted by their leader, who gave him the sele of the day and asked his name. Brian held out his passport, and after Maguire had fumbled over it and pretended that he could read, he gave it back with a grin and Brian passed on with another.

The seal of the Confederacy on the safe-conduct was quite enough for any man in these parts, however.

Brian had not ridden a hundred paces farther before he saw one of Turlough's men beckoning to him from the door of an inn, so he left his troopers to drink outside and passed within. Turlough's man joined him at a table, and there Brian gained news of the most cheering.

Six days before this the Dark Master had arrived at Swineford, with Turlough an hour behind him. The old Wolf, whose cunning made up for his lack of courage, had made shift to get two of O'Donnell's dozen men embroiled with the Maguires. The upshot of that had been a fight, followed by a delay of two days for investigation; finally the Dark Master had slipped away, his two men had promptly been hung, and Turlough had meantime gone ahead to prepare fresh delays at Bellahy and Tobercurry. He had four men left with him, though he had left Bertragh with ten.

"Then O'Donnell has four days' start of me," reflected Brian. "If Turlough can hold him, we will catch him at Sligo at latest."

He left the inn and rode back to his camp, where he had the men on the road in ten minutes. Tobercurry was only fifteen miles north, and putting his horses to a gallop, Brian rode hard and fast until that afternoon he came into the place. He found no garrison, but, instead, was met by old Turlough himself, with a bandaged head and two wounded men.

"*Mile failte!*" cried Turlough joyously, running forward to kiss Brian's hand in wild delight. "You are well come, master! Is all well down below?"

"All well, old friend," laughed Brian, swinging down to clasp the old man in his arms. "Where is the Dark Master?"

"Where we shall catch him in a forked stick presently," chuckled Turlough, wagging his beard. "Get these wild men of yours out of the town, and come into the inn with me to talk. I have all the Dark Master's plans, master, and we have only to strike."

Brian ordered his men to camp a mile outside town and to

do no plundering, so they clattered off, to the great relief of the townfolk.

"Now," said Brian, when they two were sitting across a table, "what has passed that you are bound up? Have you been fighting?"

"Well, after a fashion," grimaced Turlough disgustedly. "I was here ahead of the Dark Master, and raised the townpeople against him for a plunderer. When he came up the road was full of men; but the devil slew two and wounded two of my own men, cut his way through the rest, and as I fled north my horse flung me and bruised my head. Has the castle fallen?"

"Yes," laughed Brian, and related what had happed at Bertragh. "Have I time to bide here and eat?"

Turlough yeasaid this and sent the inn-master bustling for food and wine. When this was set before them, Turlough Wolf told his tale, beginning with the statement that two of O'Donnell's men had been captured when he cut through the townfolk and rode off.

"Where are they?" asked Brian quickly, his eyes narrowing.

"Hanged," chuckled the old man succinctly. "At Galway I could make out nothing more than the word I sent you by messenger, so I came north after O'Donnell Dubh, taking very good care that he saw nothing of me."

"I'll warrant that," laughed Brian. "We met your man at Swineford."

"Then no need to tell what passed there. Well, I said that we caught two of his men here, and I got back into the town just in time to keep the folk from hanging them to the church steeple."

"Eh?" Brian stared, with his mouth full. "Why, I thought you said—"

"*Dhar mo lamh,* give me time to finish, master!" Turlough hesitated a little, evidently in some fear. "We took them into the churchyard and burned them a little, and so got out of them all the Dark Master's plans. Then the priest shrived them, and I let the townfolk hang them."

Brian looked across the table, his blue eyes like ice and his nostrils quivering with anger; the old man slanted up his gray eyes and turned uneasily in his seat, for well he knew what Brian would say to this.

"That was ill done, Turlough Wolf. If you had not served me so well, you would repent that work. By my faith, I am minded to hang you at their side!"

Brian meant it, for the torture of men made him furious.

"I am no fool to spare mad dogs," muttered Turlough sullenly. "It was the Dark Master who lopped these ears of mine eight years gone."

"Tell your tale," said Brian curtly and fell to eating again.

"I found tidings both good and bad, master. From Galway the Dark Master had sent messengers to his kin in Donegal, bidding them send aid south; also, he sent to certain pirates north of Sligo Bay. From Sligo to the Erne all that land is desolate, and has been so these six years, and the O'Donnells from Lough Swilly have set up a pirate hold near Millhaven. It was to these that the Dark Master sent also.

"He has appointed a meeting-place in the hills beyond Drumcliff, at a certain mountain named Clochaun, or the Stone. Now, whether you think my craft evil or good, master, it is yet gainful to us."

This much Brian was forced to acknowledge, though for many days afterward he was still angry at Turlough for torturing and hanging those men. He had no scruples about a downright hanging, but torturing was a very different matter, and one of which he had tasted himself.

"Well, what is your advice in this?"

"We can do one of two things, master. The one is to ride on to Sligo and fall on him when he comes south again with his men; the other is to ride hard after him and catch him, then fall on the Millhaven men, then meet the O'Donnells who are coming south to join him at the Stone Mountain with the rest."

"The first plan is more cautious," said Brian thoughtfully;

"but to strike him when he has his men around him would be to repeat what we have done. I like the other way the better."

"It is both safer and yet more dangerous, master. Safer in that we smite him and his men separately, and more dangerous because we shall be in the heart of a wild country, without supplies, and with no aid in case we are defeated."

"It is more to my mind to talk of winning than losing," grunted Brian. "I have spare horses and money with which to buy provisions. Also, I think that I shall stamp flat that pirate nest at Millhaven, and set up my own banner there."

"Then you have a banner of your own, master?" Turlough squinted up slyly, for it was the first hint Brian had given him of what lay behind his nickname.

"Aye!" laughed Brian as the wine warmed him. "And it shall bear the Red Hand of Tyr-owen, old Wolf; but first to catch the Dark Master. Now let us go, for we shall ride to the Stone Mountain and see what haps there."

Upon that they rode forth from the town, and all the town-folk bade the crafty Turlough farewell, and gave him gifts for warning them against the "plunderers." Turlough looked up at the two bodies swinging in the wind as they passed the church-tower, and put his tongue in his cheek, but Brian said no more on the subject.

That night they camped outside the town, and Brian bought all the provision that the people would sell. This he loaded on the spare horses, and the next morning they set off for the north.

Now, in that fighting by Lough Conn, Brian had taken a shrewd clip which had reopened the bullet-tear over his scalp. Added to this, he was not yet in all of his former strength, and the hard ride to Tobercurry had set his blood to heating; wherefore it was that before coming to Sligo Brian was heavy with fever and was shaken with chill. A hard snow was driving through the night, and Turlough sent most of the men around the city to wait for them on the other side the Garravogue to avoid danger.

There was no garrison in Sligo, however. The old castle which Red Hugh O'Donnell had fought over in the old days was ruined; the grand monastery, built by Brian of Tyr-erril, had been burned by Hamilton's men, together with the town itself, and Sligo was well-nigh desolate. Turlough got shelter in a hovel, however; managed to put Brian into a miserable bed, and gave him a brew to drink. With the morning Brian found his fever gone, but weakness was on him.

They stayed in Sligo town all that day and the next night, and upon dawn, Brian insisted on riding north once more, against Turlough's protests. However, no ill came of it, for Brian was well used to riding, and the exercise gave him strength, though they made but a short march that day past the round tower of Drumcliff, halting in the hills.

As Turlough Wolf knew where the Stone Mountain was they had no use for guides. It lay only another day's march ahead of them, and there was some danger that their quarry would descry their coming and flee away to Millhaven.

"This is my rede, master;" said Turlough, "that you and I ride ahead with a few men to see how things go, and leave our men to follow. The hills are empty of rovers, for there is naught to plunder; but it were well to know if the Dark Master has joined with those friends of his."

"That seems good advice," said Brian, and, taking a dozen men, they rode forward warily, sending out other parties to scout also.

Over them towered the whiteness of the Stone Mountain, for snow lay thickly on all things. Brian gazed up at the gray-jutted crags, but his thoughts were not all with the Dark Master. Him he already accounted slain, and he was thinking of that Millhaven stronghold.

One day his own banner should fly there, he told himself. There must be a good harbor, else the northern pirates had never settled down to hold the place; and since all the country round-about lay bleak and unsettled of men, the vision came to him of first taking the place, and then fetching O'Neills from the east and north to settle the lands around. They would flock to him when his condition was made known, and that Cromwell's men would shatter the royalists and confederacy Brian saw clearly, as Owen Ruadh had foretold him.

Already the house of Tyr-owen was scattered and fallen, as the greater house of Tyr-connall had been before it, for when the last earl had fled from the land, there had been only the younger branch to hold the sept together. Owen Ruadh was the final glory of that branch, and now Brian entertained the vision of transplanting the Red Hand and of making his rule strong in the west.

But other men had entertained the same vision before him, and it had remained a vision, and no more; and the high hopes of Brian himself were fated to be driven upon the rocks of destiny before many days had passed over.

With the afternoon the little party stood on the lower slopes of the Stone Mountain itself, and Turlough drew the shape of the place in the snow with his pike-haft.

"Here are we," he explained, "on the southern slopes. A half-mile ahead of us is a valley with a small and fast-rushing water, where we shall make camp this night if the Dark Master be not before us. And if he is not, then he will be on the northern side, where there are two well-sheltered valleys with water running, fit for the meeting-place and camp of men. Here is the eastern-most, but, as I remember it, the snow fills the valley somewhat in winter. The other holds a small lake called the Dubh Linn, or Black Tarn, and in one of these we shall find the Dark Master, unless he is here before us."

"Well, let us ride on and see to that," said Brian, and they did so.

However, they found the valley deserted and empty, and picked a place for camp, sending back a horseman to bring up the force. They could make out no smoke rising from the mountain, nor dared they light fires until after dark for fear of alarming O'Donnell; but when the force came up, Brian sent out scouts to bring in what word might be had.

"Where got you such knowledge of this wilderness?" he asked Turlough that night when the fires were blazing and the men were warmed and fed. The old man narrowed his gray eyes and chuckled a little.

"I have been in many armies, master, though I have fought not; and I have been outlawed twice by the English, in the old days. This was always a good place to flee to."

Brian laughed and said no more. That night the men rested well, and Brian himself got sleep which sent strength into him and served him well in the days to come, for it was long before he was to sleep again, save as he rode, nodding in the saddle.

Not until nearly dawn did the last of the scouts straggle in. None of these bore any news, and all agreed that no signs could they find of any large band of men, nor of any men at all. Turlough heard their reports, letting Brian sleep, and only when the last man came in were any tidings brought. This man bore a strip of sheepskin, which, he said, an old woman had given him to bear to his master.

"A woman!" exclaimed Turlough, scanning the written words on the sheepskin, but unable to read them. "What is she like? It is a strange thing if women bide on Slieve Clochaun! Was there any stead near by?"

"None," replied the man, who trembled with something more than cold. *"M'anam go'n Dhia!* She was a witch woman, or worse, Turlough Wolf. She leaped out of the snow in my path, told me to bear that skin to Yellow Brian, and vanished in a burst of fire. How could she not have been a devil?"

"Nonsense!" grunted Turlough, though he suddenly laid the strip of skin down. "You are overwarm with *uisquebagh,* man. What was this woman like? Was she clad all in black?"

"Faith, I did not stop to see," grinned the man sheepishly.

Turlough stroked his beard, while the men went off to eat and sleep. He gazed at the strip of skin, and twice stretched out his hand toward it, with his eye on the fire, but each time drew back. Then he glanced around craftily, found he was alone, and took from under his cloak a small, brass crucifix. With this he touched the skin, found that nothing happened, and rose with a nod. The dawn was just breaking in the east.

"There is no sorcery in it, at least," he muttered; "but I think it bodes no great good to us. Ho, Brian!"

Brian woke and sprang up. Turlough handed him the strip of skin, saying no word, and when Brian had held it to the light of the embers, he looked up suddenly.

"Whence came this?"

"What does it say first?" returned Turlough uneasily.

"News!" cried Brian, his blue eyes aflame with eagerness. "It says that O'Donnell bides alone by the Black Tarn, and that his horsemen from the north are camped two miles beyond the mountain, waiting for him, and that he has made pact with the Millhaven pirates and they have left for their stronghold. Answer me—whence came this? It is written in good English writing, man!"

Then Turlough told of what had chanced, and when he had done, Brian stared into his gray eyes with a great wonder. Twice he tried to speak, but his lips were dry.

"The Black Woman!" he muttered thickly. "Can it be, Turlough? Who is she?"

"That was my thought, master," said Turlough. "Who she is none know save herself; but she deals with no good. This may be a trap; let us ride south again, and at once, lest evil come upon us."

"South? Not I," laughed Brian, though his face was pale. "To horse, men!"

And at his ringing shout the camp awoke, and Brian saw his vengeance drawing near.

CHAPTER XV

WHAT HAPPENED AT THE TARN

IT HAD been long, indeed, since Brian had given thought to his meeting with the Black Woman on the other side of Ireland. In that brief meeting, the Black Woman had spoken of seeing the old earl, his grandfather, in his youth. Yet it was forty years since the two earls, O'Donnell and O'Neill, had fled together from Ireland, and even then Tyr-owen had been an old man. Unless this Black Woman was close on a hundred years of age, Brian could not see how she had known Hugh O'Neill in his youth.

The mere fact that she had recognized him there in the moonlight was proof of her true speaking, however. Brian could no longer hide from himself that her words had some strange prophecy in them. She had foretold his meeting with Cathbarr and with the Bird Daughter, though, indeed, she might have been attempting only to guide him on the path which he had afterward followed.

While the men were saddling, Brian called Turlough and told of the hag's word that she would meet him again "on a black day for him."

"Now, what think you she meant by that, Turlough? Is this the meeting?"

"No, master, for it is no meeting. It may be as you think, and that she was but trying to lead you into the west; yet, for my part, I call it sorcery," and the old man crossed himself, for, like better men than himself, Turlough ascribed all he could not fathom to magic. "It seems to me that she is some witch who is hanging on your tracks, and that when—"

"Oh, nonsense!" laughed Brian, flinging the matter from his mind. "At any rate, she has served me well this time. Now, what rede shall we follow in this matter, and shall we capture and slay the Dark Master first, or fall on his men first, or both together?"

"It is ill to sunder a force of men, master," quoth Turlough. "If those horsemen of O'Donnell's are encamped in a valley two miles to the north, it is a vale of which I know well. But we must mind this—if O'Donnell gets safe into Galway again with either these horsemen or those Millhaven pirates of his clan, he will drive hard against Bertragh."

"The Dark Master shall come no more to Galway," said Brian grimly, fingering his ax. "Now finish, and quickly."

"I have a plan in my mind, master; but unless we slay the Dark Master, it is like to fail us. Let us send a hundred of the men around to the north, for I will tell them how to ride, so that by this night they can fall upon those men of his and scatter them in the darkness, and drive them south where we can slay them utterly at our wills. If we drove them back whence they came, there would be little craft in it, and it is to my liking to do a thing well or not at all."

"A true word there," nodded Brian, his eyes gleaming. "I think those men are as good as dead now, Turlough. Speak on."

"With fifty men, master, you and I can reach the valley of the Dubh Linn. We cannot do it with horses, unless we ride around to the north, and in that there would be danger of striking on the Dark Master's scouts. But while our hundred are circling far around, we with fifty can go over the mountain by valleys and paths I know of, so that by this evening we will come to the Black Tarn and strike the Dark Master as our hundred men fall on his camp. That is my—"

"Good!" cried Brian, leaping up eagerly. "Then we—"

"Hold, master!" And Turlough caught his arm, quickly staying him. When Brian looked down he read a sudden fear in the old man's gray eyes. "That was my first rede, Yellow Brian, and you would do well to hear my second also."

"Say it," said Brian, and glanced at the brightening sky.

"My second rede is this. That message might be a trap to ensnare us, though I have two minds about this Black Woman. But if we fail to slay the Dark Master at the Black Tarn, we are like to have an ill time."

"Why so?" asked Brian, for he could see no likelihood of that. "I said that we would slay him."

"Master, do you hold the lives of men in your keeping?" In the gray eyes leaped a swift horror that amazed Brian. "I tell you that if the Dark Master escapes from our hand, and his men are driven past our fifty into the south, he will ride hard before us into Galway. I see evil in that first rede of mine, Yellow Brian. I see evil in it—"

He broke off, staring past Brian with fixed and unseeing eyes, his face rigid.

"Turlough, are you mad?" Brian seized the other's shoulder, shaking him harshly. The old man shivered a little, and sanity came back into his eyes as they met the icy blue of Brian's. "What daftness is upon you, man?"

"I know not, master," whimpered old Turlough feebly. "Do as you will."

"Then I will to follow your rede, divide my men as you say, and when we have slain the Dark Master, we will cut off the last of these O'Donnells of his, ride to Millhaven and take that hold, and send word to the Bird Daughter that she may keep Bertragh Castle and send Cathbarr north to me. Now go, and tell a hundred of the men how to ride around this mountain; then be ready to guide me over it to the Black Tarn."

"You are a hard man, Yellow Brian," said Turlough, and turned him about and did as Brian had ordered.

None the less, Brian gave some thought to that second rede of Turlough's. He saw clearly enough that with the northern horsemen driven past, scattered though they might be, they could be cut off to a man if the Dark Master were slain. But if O'Donnell should escape by some trick of fate, he could gather up his men and drive south.

"If he does that, there will be slaying between Sligo and Galway," swore Brian quickly. "But I cannot see that he will escape me here. When another day breaks, I shall have won my Spanish blade again—and then ho! for the Red Hand of Tyr-owen!"

So Brian laughed and donned his jack and back-piece, while Turlough drew plans in the snow and showed the leaders of the hundred how to sweep around without discovery so that they might fall on the northern horsemen at eve.

Brian had grown into an older and grimmer man since the day he had stood beside the bed of Owen Ruadh O'Neill, short though the time had been. Youth was still in his face when he smiled out, but suffering had deepened his eyes and sunk his cheeks and drawn the skin tighter over that powerful jaw of his. When he had armed, he stood in thought for a little, with hand on jaw in his instinctive gesture, and wakened suddenly to find old Turlough bending the knee before him.

"Now I know of what blood you come, Yellow Brian," said the old man softly. "I saw Hugh O'Neill, the great earl, standing even as you stand now, on the morning when we slew the English at the Yellow Ford."

"Man, man!" exclaimed Brian in wonder; "that battle was fought fifty years ago, and yet you say that you were there?"

"I was the earl's horse-boy, master." And Brian saw tears on the old man's beard. "I loved him, and I was at the flight of the earls ten years after, going with Tyr-owen to Italy, and it was these hands laid him in his grave, master; master, have faith in me—"

Brian put down his hands to those of Turlough, his heart strangely softened.

"He was my grandfather," he said simply, and Turlough broke down and wept like a child.

When they left their horses and the camp behind, Brian followed Turlough, feeling like a new man. He had lightened his heart of a great load, and he wished that he had talked of these things with Turlough Wolf long before this. Now he understood why the old man had offered him service as he stood in that attitude on the battlements of O'Reilly's castle after leaving Owen Ruadh, and he understood the love that Turlough bore him, and the silence the old man had kept on the matter, though it must have ever been deep in his heart to speak out.

No more words passed between them, nor did Brian tell Turlough more of his story until long after; but of this there was no need. As they climbed higher on the mountain they could see the hundred horsemen filing off to the eastward; but soon these were lost sight of as Turlough led Brian and the fifty through the valleys and deep openings, which were drifted deep in snow, making progress slow and wearisome.

Indeed, Brian thought afterward that this hard traveling might have been responsible for what chanced on the other side of the mountain.

On the higher crests and ridges there was little snow, however, and Turlough seemed to know every inch of the place by heart, though more than once Brian gave himself up for lost in the maze of smaller peaks and the twisted paths they followed. Most of the fifty Turlough had chosen from those hillmen who had joined Brian by Lough Conn, so that they were not unused to such climbing, and remained with spirits unshaken by the vast loneliness that surrounded them, and to which other men might have succumbed somewhat.

Brian himself was no little awed by the desolate grandeur of the Stone Mountain, but he only wrapped his cloak more closely about him, and swore that the Dark Master should yield up the Spanish blade before many more hours.

And so indeed it was done, though not as Brian looked for.

Until long after noon the band wended their way with great toil and pain over the flanks of the mountain, until Turlough led Brian out to a point of black rock and motioned toward the valleys below them.

"There to the left," he said, "is the valley of the Black Tarn. Do you see that smoke, Brian, and that dark spot between the trees and the lake?"

Brian looked, squinting because of the snow-glare. Leading down from the side of the mountain itself was a valley—long, and widening gradually to the plain, where a dark wood swallowed it up. Almost under his feet, as it were, was a small, round lake deep in the rock, with a small, frozen-over outlet that was lost in the snow.

But farther down the valley-slopes there were trees, and among them horses tethered and a fire strewing smoke on the air close beside. Between this little wood and the tarn itself there stood a low house of thatch with smoke also rising from it, and from the other fire among the trees came a sheen of steel caps and jacks, where were men.

But to Brian all these things were very small and hard to make out distinctly, as if he were looking at some carven mimicry, such as children are wont to use in play.

"Now come," said Turlough Wolf. "It is no easy task getting there without being discovered, and the way is long."

Brian found, indeed, that to avoid being seen from below they must needs take a roundabout way; but when the afternoon was far spent they had come to a snow-filled hollow among the rocks which Turlough declared was just over the edge of that valley-slope where stood the low house. Turlough said that in his day that house had not stood there, and he knew nothing of it.

Since there could be no talk of lighting a fire, Brian's men huddled together in the hollow, and ate and drank cheerlessly. Brian was minded to meet the Dark Master and win his Spanish blade with his own hand, so he ordered that his men pass on after dark and make ready to fall upon those men who were camped at the wood, but to hold off until he and Turlough had smitten the Dark Master in that little thatched house, where he was most like to be found. Turlough yeasaid this plan, for he trusted greatly to Brian's strength.

At length they set out under the cold stars, and Brian's men were very weary, but promised to do all as he had commanded. He and Turlough set off alone over the hill, and when they had come to the hill-crest after much toiling through the snow they looked down and found the house a hundred yards below them.

"Let us go down cautiously," said Turlough, "for I think we can peer through the thatch and plan our stroke well."

So they struck down openly across the hill-slope, and found that there was none on guard. The door of the house was fast shut, but Turlough strode cautiously in the trampled snow around the house, where, at the side, a spark of firelight glittered through the loose thatch. To this he led Brian, and Brian stooped down and looked through the cranny, while Turlough went farther and fared as well.

There was but one room in the hut, and it was well lighted by the fire that glittered merrily on the hearth. Sitting not far away, but with his back to Brian, was a man; he sat on a stool, and there seemed to be a wide earthenware bowl of water or some dark liquid on the floor between his feet into which he was staring. In his bent-down position his rounded shoulders stood up stark against the fire, and Brian knew this was the Dark Master.

His hand went to the pistol in his belt, but since there was no other man in the hut, he thought it shame to murder O'Donnell as he sat, and made up his mind to go around to the door and burst in. He saw his own great sword slung across the Dark Master's back, but even as he stirred to rise, O'Donnell's voice came to him, low and vibrant, so that he bode where he was and listened.

"I cannot make out the figures," muttered the Dark Master, still staring down into the bowl of dark water. "The man has the face of Yellow Brian, yet he is swart; the woman I sure never saw before. *Corp na diaoul!* What is the meaning of this? Who stands in my way?"

Brian paused in no little astonishment, and stole a glance aside to see old Turlough crossing himself fervently. It struck his mind that he had chanced on some sorcery here, and, remembering the tales he had heard of the Dark Master's work, he laughed a little and settled down. He was minded to see what this thing might be; but he made his pistol ready in case the magic told O'Donnell of his danger.

"It is some great man," came the Dark Master's voice again. "There is something broidered on his— By my soul, it is the Red Hand of Tyr-owen! It is The O'Neill himself—the earl— Is Yellow Brian of his blood, then?"

At hearing this Brian crouched closer, in some fear and more wonder. Was the Dark Master in reality seeing such figures in that water-bowl? Then the man must be either mad or—or figures were there. Now O'Donnell's voice rose stronger:

"Which of these twain stands now in my way? It is not Yellow Brian. Ah, the earl is slipping away, and the woman is smiling. One of his loves, belike, for he had many; she is fair, wondrous fair! Ah, what's this?"

Brian saw the dark figure crouch lower, as if in astonishment.

"Changing, changing! Is it this woman who stands in my way, then? Toothless and grinning, crouched low over a stick, rags and tatters and wisps of gray hair—"

The Dark Master paused in his jerky speech, stiffened as if in wild amazement at that which he beheld, and a sudden cry broke from him, sharp and awestruck:

"The Black Woman!"

Then Brian straightened up, feeling Turlough's hand touch his; but for a space he stood silent while his mind cast out for what the Dark Master's words meant.

In a flash it came to him. Through some black dealings O'Donnell had in truth pictured The O'Neill in that bowl, and with him a woman he had loved and who loved him; and this was no other than she whom Brian had known as the Black Woman, now become an old hag indeed, with only the memories of her fair youth and her love behind her. And this was why she had recognized him and why she had evidently watched over him since that first meeting, out of the love she had borne the earl, his grandsire, in days now buried under many bitter years.

The two men looked into each other's eyes, and Brian saw that Turlough's jaw had dropped loosely, and that fright had stricken the old man almost out of his senses. With that Brian felt his own fear take wings. He laughed a little as his grip closed on the haft of his ax, and the cold star-glint seemed to shine back again from his eyes.

"Bide here if you will," he smiled quietly. "I have my work to do."

And, turning with the word, he strode quickly to the door, just as there came a great cry from within the place.

CHAPTER XVI

BRIAN GETS HIS SWORD AGAIN

BRIAN PUSHED the door open, and it gave easily to his fist. Gazing within he saw the Dark Master standing over the shattered bowl, whose liquid flowed down toward the hearth and hissed on the embers; plainly, the Dark Master had seen nothing good in that water, for he had shattered the bowl with his foot, and his teeth were snarling under his drooping mustache.

"I am come," said Brian, laughing grimly as he stood in the doorway.

O'Donnell whirled, gripping at his sword.

Now, whether there was magic on the place, as Turlough ever swore, or whether the opening of the door had made a draft, as Brian thought more likely, a strange thing happened.

Brian had raised his pistol in his left hand, meaning to kill the Dark Master without pity in that first moment. Out of the hearth came a great swirl of ashes and red embers, flying toward the door and closing around O'Donnell; as Brian pressed the trigger the ashes smote him in a blinding swirl, and a harsh laugh answered the roar of the pistol.

With a curse Brian cleared his eyes of the light ash and reached with his ax at the dim figure of the Dark Master, nigh hid with ashes and powder-smoke. From down the vale came other shots and cries, and he knew his men had struck on that small camp lying there; but at this O'Donnell gave him other things to think of.

That was a great fight, for Brian was little used to ax-play and had much ado to parry the keen thrusts of his own Spanish blade; the roof was too low to give room for a swing, and when the Dark Master had lunged him back to the door again, he knew that he had done ill. So with another bitter curse Brian flung the ax from his hand and ripped out the long, Irish dagger that hung at his girdle.

For all his wrath he had taken good heed to fling the ax aright, and the broad flat of it took the Dark Master full in the chest and bore him back, reeling and shouting for his men. Before he could recover Brian leaped at him, caught O'Donnell's sword wrist in his left hand, and aimed a deadly stroke with his *skean.*

The blow went true, but the steel turned aside from the Dark Master's mail-shirt; O'Donnell caught his wrist in turn, and there the two stood heaving each at the other for a long minute. Brian's eyes struck cold and hard into the evil features of the Dark Master; the other's breath came hot on his cheeks, and so beastlike was the man's face that Brian half expected those snarling teeth to close snapping at his throat. But the Dark Master was strong, for all his hunched shoulders.

Then a great flame of vengeance seemed to cleave Brian's soul, and with a curt laugh he threw out his strength and flung the Dark Master back bodily so that he fell into the hearth and burst the mud chimney and the thatched wall behind. Before he could rise again Brian had whipped out his other pistol and fired; he saw the man's figure writhe aside, then up through the powder-smoke rose a burning brand that smote him over the brow heavily. At the same instant the scattered sparks caught the thatch, and the whole house broke into flame.

Brian's eyes found the dark figure once more and he rushed forward. At the broken heap of mud from the chimney his feet struck on the sword, which had fallen from the Dark Master's hand, and he caught it up with a cry of joy and bore forward.

That brief instant of delay lost him his quarry, however. Brian flung through the shattered wall, with the whole structure flaming up behind him; he saw a dark figure on the snow and ran at it, only to find himself striking at Turlough Wolf, and stayed his hand barely in time.

"Where is he?" he panted hoarsely, looking around with fierce eyes.

Then he caught the Dark Master's figure running across the snow toward that camp amid the trees, where fighting was still forward and men were shouting and firing. Brian rushed off, with Turlough staggering after him; but with a sob of despairing anger he saw the Dark Master flit into the trees, and heard his voice ringing at his men.

It turned out afterward that Brian's fifty men, weary and chilled, had made a somewhat heartless assault on the score of horsemen camped in the trees; therefore, instead of carrying O'Donnell's men off their feet and cutting them down straightway, they were held off for a little.

The Dark Master knew that he was lost if he stayed long in that place, however, and when Brian reached the clump of trees he found that he was too late. With two or three men behind him, O'Donnell had cut through Brian's men and was galloping away. Brian groaned savagely, leaped at a mounted man and dragged him from the saddle, and was just springing up when Turlough caught and stayed him.

"Wait, master!" panted the old man in desperate fear of the surging men around him, but in more desperate fear for Brian. "This is madness, for I ordered our fifty horses fetched around—"

"Bide here for them, then!" said Brian, and swung up into the saddle. One of the Dark Master's men barred his way, and Brian's blade went through his throat; then he was off after the four figures who by now were far distant toward the dark forest that swallowed up the valley ahead.

The cold night air cleared his brain, however, and after a moment he drew rein with bitterness upon him. Turlough had spoken rightly, for to ride after those four men with his naked sword alone was in truth madness. So he came back again to where the last of the hemmed-in horsemen was being cut out of his saddle, and when his men gathered about him with a shout, his tongue gave them little joy.

"You are fools," he said harshly, "for the Dark Master has escaped us. Take these horses, fifteen of you, and ride. Let five men go to bring in our horses with all speed, and let ten more scatter out in search of our hundred men. These are not more than two miles distant, and in an hour I must ride from here. See to it that you return with the men and horses by then, or shift for yourselves."

"That is too much," spoke out a burly fellow angrily. "We have been climbing all day, and have——"

Brian said no word, but leaned down from his saddle and his Spanish blade flickered in the light. The man fell and lay quiet, while the others drew back in black fear.

"I am master here," said Brian coldly, when a long instant had passed. "Go."

There was no more muttering among his recruits, either then or later. He dismounted, saw that the O'Donnells had been slain to the last man, and joined Turlough at the campfire. Food and drink had been found in the camp, and a flagon of wine heartened Brian greatly.

"Now give me your rede, Turlough Wolf," he said. "I have failed in this matter, and it seems that ill shall come of it."

"So I foretold, master, but we may still remedy the ill if we catch O'Donnell. I think that by now his horsemen are scattered, and this burning hut will draw our own men thither. Before midnight they will be here, and we can ride forth. I think that the Dark Master will gather what men are left him and strike down for Galway."

"Two men may ride the same road," quoth Brian grimly, and set his naked blade in his belt. He saw that before him lay some fighting and much hard riding, so inside the next hour he had his men full-fed. Before this was finished the spare horses and those of his men came in, for Turlough had ordered them to start at noon and ride around in case of need.

Brian determined to spare neither men nor horseflesh on that riding, and when his men were mounted he set out across the night to meet his hundred, and to hear what had been done at the camp two miles distant. As the moon was rising he met them; and if he was glad at the meeting, they were twice glad.

They had found the camp and had lain off it until after dark as Turlough had bidden them, the more so since there were two-score over a hundred men there. But at length they had ridden down as if they were fresh come from the north, and had twice ridden through the camp before the O'Donnells were well awake, though it had been sharp work. The result had been that a score of Brian's men had fallen, they had slain a full half of the O'Donnells, and the rest had been driven and scattered southward. Brian's men had plundered their camp and were weary, so that when they heard of what had chanced at the Black Tarn they were somewhat less than half willing to ride farther.

But Brian speedily persuaded them to that course, and Turlough led them all to the south on the way to Sligo.

Bitterness and heaviness of heart dwelt deep in Brian that night, and for some time to come. With the escape of the Dark Master, whether it had been by magic or craft, all his visions had burst; he must ride away from the pirate hold at Millhaven, he saw that he would lose many men on his way south, and yet there lay no choice before him. He had scotched the snake, and now he must kill it. If the Dark Master reached Galway town in safety, those O'Donnells from Millhaven would be around by sea to meet him, and the royalists would lend him men and guns to go against Bertragh in their cause.

"Is there any likelihood that the Dark Master will miss those scattered men of his?" he asked Turlough, who rode on his right hand.

"Little, master. There is but the one road south to Sligo at this season, and it is great wonder indeed that the scattered men did not fall on us at the Black Tarn in seeking their master. But with only seventy-five men or so I do not think they will bide our coming."

"Nor do I," and Brian laughed grimly as he thought of that fight with his enemy.

Certain men had been wounded in those frays, and he left them to follow after him, so that he turned south with a hundred and a score men at his back. He did not think that the Dark Master would face him, but since those men were all O'Donnells who would obey him utterly, he looked to have some fighting; in which he was not far wrong.

An hour after the day was broken they thundered up to the bridge that spanned the Garravogue, and ten wild and silent men were holding that bridge behind an overturned cart for barricade. Brian would waste no men on a storm, but slew six of the men with musketry and rode over the other four; even so, those four brought down three of his men before they were done with.

Brian baited the horses in Sligo, remaining there a scant half-hour. From the townfolk he learned that the Dark Master was but two hours ahead of him, and Brian had great hopes of running him to earth that same day. So he set forth again and they rode hard to Ballsadare, at the south branch of Sligo Bay, and on to Coolany at the edge of the Storm Mountains.

At this latter place they found different work, however, for here was a small garrison of Cavan pikemen who stopped them, lined with their pikes three deep across the road before the church. Brian was no long time in learning that the Dark Master had spread word of him as a plunderer and Parliament man.

"I have no time to waste on you," he said shortly to the leader of the pikemen. "Here is a safe-conduct, and I am Stephen Burke."

"None the less, you must stay until I have looked into this," said the other, pulling out his pistol with some determination.

"Stay I will not, but I think you shall," replied Brian, and thrust as the man fired. The bullet glanced from his jack, but the officer fell back among his pikes, and Brian spurred after him in great anger. His Scots troopers were in the van, or what was left of them, and they came down galloping, and rode over the pikemen leaving a sea of smitten men in the roadway behind.

Also, ten of Brian's men were left.

By the evening they were back at Tobercurry again, where Turlough had hung those two men after torturing them. The Dark Master was something over an hour ahead of them, and he had stayed to fire the church and the town. Brian's heart was sore for the townfolk, but he could pause no longer than to bait horses and men, since he looked for hard riding that night; however, he gave what money and plunder he had to the townfolk and got a blessing in return, and so rode forth again as the stars peeped out.

"There are Maguires in Swineford, master," said old Turlough with a cunning, sidelong look.

"I met them coming north," laughed Brian softly. "They will prove good men to avoid, so I think that we shall ride around that burg."

Brian thought that he could get through the Maguires, but he intended to take no chances. However, they had gained to within five miles of Swineford and had halted to blow the horses, when one of the scouts came riding back to say that a score of farmers with three carts were approaching from the town.

Presently they came on them—a black mass swinging down the road, which was very boggy on either hand. Neither Brian nor Turlough smelt any ill in this until they were within a hundred paces of the party, when suddenly the carts were swung across the road and a score of muskets spat death into Brian's men.

"Back!" shouted Brian, when his men would have charged. "We have no time and lives to waste on this party—what shall we do, Turlough? The fields are all bog."

"We cannot well ride around," said Turlough, when they had

ridden back a little, leaving dead men on the road. "But a little way back is a path that leads out and around Swineford. Put ten men here to keep these O'Donnells from following us, and we will make a short cut to the Moy near Kiltanmugh. It was a clever trick, this!"

It was indeed, and it had cost Brian a round score of men, so that he followed Turlough out into the open land with less than a hundred men behind him. His fury abated before dawn, when they had splashed across the Moy and came upon the road once more, but he saw that the O'Donnells were willing enough to die if the Dark Master might escape, and he became more cautious.

When the night fell again they were far south of Claremorris, but a score of horses had foundered and he was forced to leave more men behind. Until evening Turlough led him at a distance from the main roads, then they struck into good riding again and save for one detour to avoid Tuam would have a clear road between themselves and Galway, which Brian meant to reach before dawn unless his own horse foundered with the rest.

Of the Dark Master they heard nothing until they were ford-ing the Clare north of Tuam, when two men gave them word that a scant half-hour before some two-score horsemen had fled past them toward Tuam.

"Good!" cried Brian. "Now, Turlough, lead us around Tuam, and I think we shall finish this thing long before the day comes."

Said Turlough sourly, "Every horse down is a man gone, master," but to that Brian only laughed and set in his spurs.

So now they let gallop through the darkness, trusting more to Turlough's wits than to their horses' feet; for Brian knew that if his own beasts were spent, those of the Dark Master were no better unless he were to get mounts at Tuam. That would be hard, however, for there were no horses to be had save far in the mountains where the war had not swept all things away.

No sooner had they reached the road again beyond Tuam than it seemed to Brian that he heard the faint drum of hoofs ahead of him, and at that he gave a shout and drove on with such of his men storming behind as might come. Many of them had gone down, indeed, but now all wakened from their nodding sleep and kept close, though here and there one dropped out. Turlough, whose steed had been the best of all save Brian's, kept at his master's flank.

They were hard on Claregalway when Brian saw his quarry first—a deep mass of men far ahead on an open stretch of road. Then he knew that the race was nearly won, and for all that his beast was sobbing under his thighs, he raced ahead, and laughed out loud when a little band cut off from the main body of the Dark Master's men. There were fifteen or less who waited his coming with pistols ready, but Brian rode hardily at them, their balls whistled overhead or past, and he was on them.

The shock of the meeting came near to unseating him, and sent one of the foe sprawling, horse and man; Brian cut another to the chin and thrust the life from a third, and before the first sword had slithered on his steel-cap his men had swept aside the devoted fifteen, and he was riding on. O'Donnell had straightened his party for nothing.

Now the Dark Master was riding for his life, and knew it. Some few of his men fell out with spent beasts, and these Brian's party rode over, taking and giving but one blow, or none at all. When Claregalway drew up ahead, cold and gray under the stars, Brian was but two hundred yards behind with forty men still behind him, while O'Donnell had not half so many.

As he thundered down to the river Brian had drawn as much ahead of Turlough and the others as he was behind the Dark Master. He shouted back to those of his men whose matches were lit to loose off their muskets, but before the first pan had flashed out he saw the O'Donnells draw rein and wheel at the bridge-head, while two of their number drove clattering on into the town.

Now, had Brian chosen to wait for his men things would have fallen out differently; but this he would not do, for he thought to break through these as he had done with the others. So he went at them with naked sword, his heart raging within him and his face set and cold like stone. He was still fifty paces from the bridge-head when their pistols spattered out; the men behind dared not fire for fear of hitting him, so that Brian had all the fight for himself.

He came near to having none, for at that first discharge a pistol-ball split his jack and lodged in his buff-coat over his heart, while another came between his arm and his side, drawing blood a little from both; while a third and worse went into his horse between the fore shoulders. Brian felt the poor beast falter shudderingly, and pause; then the O'Donnells shouted greatly and closed about him, thinking to slay him before his men could come up.

Brian saw a long *skean* plunge into his horse's neck, and in terrible anger he smote with the edge, so that a hand and arm hung down from the dagger, a ghastly thing to see. But the poor steed was dead with that blow, and Brian had but time to fling himself headlong ere the horse rolled over.

The leap saved his life, for the O'Donnells were striking fast at him. Brian rose up between two of them, dragged one down with his left hand and thrust the other under the arm, and tried to leap up into the saddle. But as he did so his own men struck, so that the horses were swept together and pinned Brian's legs between them, and he hung helpless.

In that instant he saw an ax swinging above him and flung back his head, but not enough, for the ax fell, and Brian went down under the horses.

Save for three of his men who saw the thing and stood over him, Brian would have been trampled to death on the spot. These O'Donnells were no loose fighting-men, and they smote shrewdly against the press of Brian's greater numbers, while their wild cry rose high over the shrill of steel. When Brian's men knew that he was down, however, they struck such blows as they knew not they had in them, and quarter was not asked or offered in that battle by the bridge.

The fight was not ended until the last O'Donnell went down in a swirl and clash of steel. Then Turlough, who had kept well out of it according to his wont, pushed through and fell upon Brian's body. When Brian opened his eyes his head was still ringing, while his men were bathing him with water. After an instant he sat up and gazed around.

"The Dark Master—did you catch him?"

"Nay, our thought was all for you, master," answered Turlough.

Brian groaned in great bitterness, but said no word. He knew that his chance was gone from him for that time, and as he looked around his heart sank within him. Half of his men had slipped down and lay sleeping among the dead, and the rest could scarce stay in their saddles for weariness and lack of sleep. But Turlough sprang up and gazed at the graying sky with fear in his face.

"Up, master!" he cried fiercely. "We must still ride hard, for the Dark Master will send out a troop of horse from Galway to catch us, and we must get past that town before the sun is high!"

So the sleeping were roused in haste, the wounded were put in saddle, and with their beasts staggering under them, those that were left of Brian's men closed around him and rode over the bridge through Claregalway.

CHAPTER XVII

BRIAN GOES A CRUISING

ABOVE THE head of Bertraghboy Bay there was a swooping curve in the hill road. It was at this same curve that Brian Buidh had first met the Dark Master, and it was here he had set that trap which had won him tribute for the Bird Daughter. When first he had ridden that road Brian had had a score of lusty men at his back; on the second occasion he had headed a hundred and four-score; but when he drew rein there a week after that fight at Claregalway bridge there was with him only old Turlough Wolf, and their horses were sorry skeletons like themselves.

"We are somewhat worse than when we twain started out together," laughed Brian bitterly. "Then we had full bellies at the least, but now we have naught."

"There are men coming, master," said Turlough, hanging weakly to his saddle. "I think they are our castle watchers."

Very gaunt was Brian that day, and nigh spent with his wounds and hunger and weariness. During the week that had passed since the Dark Master slipped away from him, nothing but evil had come upon him.

First they had tried to slip past to the north of the city, and had reached the Lough Corrib River, and could even faintly hear the bells of St. Nicholas below, when a half-troop of horse fell upon them. Then in desperation Brian's men smote for the last time, and put the royalists to flight; but there Brian lost the most of his men. However, he got fresh horses, and so fled eastward again when more men were seen approaching.

What chanced in the six days following is not fully set forth, for Brian got little glory from it. One by one he lost his men, and at length was forced north again to the shores of Lough Corrib, with men riding hot and fast to catch him. With Turlough Wolf alone left to him, he had made shift to cross the lake in a leaky fisherman's boat, the horses swimming behind, and so came into the O'Flahertys' country.

There word had also gone forth against him, but because of the pact between them, Murrough of the Kine sped him in peace through Iar Connaught, and at length Brian had won home again with joyless heart.

As Turlough said, men were coming, and they were Brian's own men who watched the roads. From them he got food and wine and two fresh horses, and with the afternoon they rode down to Bertragh in worse shape than they had ridden from it. Brian was the less heartened when he saw two of Nuala O'Malley's ships in the bay, and knew that she must be at the castle.

Indeed, before they reached the gates the Bird Daughter rode out to meet them, with Cathbarr striding before her. When the woman saw Brian's face her violet eyes filled with tears, and when he dismounted and kissed her hand and would have spoken, she stayed him.

"Nay, we know enough of the story for now, Brian. First rest and eat, then talk."

Brian guessed straightway that pigeons had come from her men in Galway telling of those ridings about the city, and that she had come over to Bertragh in anxiety; and this was the truth indeed.

Turlough Wolf hied him away and slept, but Brian sat about a table in the hall with Cathbarr and Nuala. He was very worn and weary, but when he had eaten and drunk he refused to sleep yet a while, and told how that storm had fared north and what had come of it.

"So I have lost a hundred and fifty hard-won men," he concluded gloomily. "I would not grudge them if the Dark Master had fallen, but he is in Galway, and the Millhaven pirates will be down to meet him, and that means war on Bertragh."

"I will be glad of that," said Cathbarr simply. "I am sound again and have been sharpening up this ax of mine."

Nuala smiled and put her hand across the table to lay it on Brian's.

"Success would be of little worth, Yellow Brian," she said softly, and her eyes steadied him, "if it were won without reverses. Few men have the luck to win always, and a touch of defeat is not an ill thing, perhaps. When we had this news of you from Galway, a week since, I sent off a galley to find Blake at the Cove of Cork and seek aid of him. Also my kinsmen will return to Gorumna before going home to Erris, and we are not in hard case here. So now get rested, Brian Buidh, and afterward we will see what may be done. Those Millhaven men have not yet passed Erris, or I would have word of it by pigeon, so they have doubtless delayed to plunder in Sligo or Killala."

Brian looked into her eyes, and from that moment he began to put behind him all thoughts of capturing that Millhaven castle for himself or of placing himself out of touch with Nuala O'Malley. He went to his chamber as she bade, and slept that night and the next day and the night after, waking on the second morning still empty of sleep and seeming more weary than when he had laid down.

This was but seeming, however, and when he had bathed and eaten he felt more like himself than for many a day.

Cathbarr had departed at dawn with a wagon-load of powder to trade for kine with his O'Flaherty kinsmen in the hills, and before Brian had broken his fast one of the galleys from Gorumna came over with three pigeons for Nuala. The cage was brought to her as she sat at meat with Brian in the hall, and

she opened the tiny messages with all the delighted anticipa-
tion of a girl.

"This is from that galley I sent to Cork," she exclaimed, laying
down the first. "It merely reports safe arrival and the delivery
of my letter to Blake, who is leaving there before long. Now for
the—ah!"

"Good news or bad?" smiled Brian easily, as animation flashed
into her face. She looked up at him with a rippling laugh.

"Both, Brian! This is from Erris, and says that the O'Donnell
seamen have made a landing at Ballycastle under Downpatrick
Head, and will likely put to sea again in a day or two. They will
give Erris a wide berth, never fear, and that means that they will
make no pause until they come to Galway."

The third message was from Galway itself, and said that the
Dark Master was biding the coming of those Millhaven men,
and had been promised both horsemen and shot if they came,
so that Bertragh might be taken and held for Ireland against
the Parliament.

"It is not taken yet," laughed Nuala as old Turlough came
shuffling up, and they gave him the sele of the day merrily
enough. "You had best keep these birds, Brian, so that if there
is any need you may send me messages to Gorumna. Now, shall
we bide here until the Dark Master comes against us?"

"I thought you were going to take me cruising with you?"
smiled Brian, but at that Turlough struck in and asked what
the messages were. When he had heard them he stood pulling
at his gray beard for a little, then turned to Brian.

"How is your body, master?"

"Well enough," said Brian, feeling his head. "Save for this
beard, which now I may not cut for a time."

He intended to abide by that oath of his, and so his beard was
growing out and his hair as well, of which latter he was glad.

Since he had ever kept his face clean shaven, however, the
beard was not to his liking. He was quite unaware that it built
out his face greatly and made him grimmer-looking than before,

and yet so young were his blue eyes except when he was in anger that it was not hard for Nuala to believe that he was only two years older than herself.

None the less, she made great sport of his beard, saying that it curled at the end like a drake's tail, as indeed it did; and as Brian only repaid her laughter with the open wonder and admiration that he held for her, there was great good-comradeship between them.

"There is still one chance for stopping the Dark Master," said Turlough thoughtfully. "If we cut off those pirate ships on their way south he is not like to get much help from Galway."

"Oh—and I never thought of it!" cried Nuala, staring at him.

Turlough chuckled. "That was spoken like a woman, mistress! If the rede seems good we could lay aboard men from here for fighting, and sail out with those two ships of yours."

Now Brian's heart filled with new hope, and after no long discussion they decided to adopt the plan. Nuala was of the opinion that a short cruise would do Brian great good, so they decided to set off that evening in her two ships, leaving Turlough to keep the castle against Cathbarr's return.

Had they taken Turlough Wolf with them or had Brian been less close-mouthed on his return from that cruise, the evil that befell might have been averted. The old man was cunning and swift at piercing beneath the craft of other men and turning it back upon themselves; but as Brian's mind lost its bitterness at his own failure it gained joy at being with the Bird Daughter, while Nuala had no less friendship and liking for him, so that neither of them gave much thought to O'Donnell Dubh who lay in Galway and bided his time after his own fashion.

Once having reached their decision, they hastened it somewhat and sent men and muskets aboard the two ships at noon. Nuala wished to sail first to Gorumna Castle and make all safe there, then reach back for Slyne Head. She proposed that Brian take one carack and she the other, but at this Brian laughed.

"No, lady—I am no seaman, and I am your guest on this cruise, so I go with you."

"Well, you shall have good guesting," she answered, flushing a little, but her eyes not flinching from his, and so they went aboard her ship together.

Having two hundred men still, Brian had put fifty on each ship in case they met with those pirates, who were like to give good battle. Also Turlough had hopes that many of Brian's men would win home from that riding of his yet, since a large part of them had dropped out by the way or had been left behind with wounds. And in the end, indeed, fifty or less did find their way back.

Before night they made Gorumna Castle, and Brian found why they had come here first. With her Kerry recruits, Nuala had a hundred and eighty men, so she had set to work to build a tower and small keep on the opposite island, that Gorumna itself might be more easily defended. Also she had taken some falconets and two bastards out of a large French ship, and had set about building a battery outside the castle that would overlook the harbor.

"That will be better than good when it is done," said Brian approvingly. "But you had best get it done speedily. When we come back from this cruise you shall take this hundred men of mine, for I will not need them until the Dark Master comes, and of that we shall have good warning."

This she was glad of, and she was glad because Brian had found her work well planned; nor did either of them suspect what grief that loan of a hundred men was to bring upon Brian.

They paused only to sup at Gorumna, then set forth again, and by dawn were off Slyne Head with a light breeze behind them. Nuala would take no chance of missing those Millhaven men, so instead of going north among the islands she turned her ships and beat off Slyne all that day, seeing no sail save fishing-craft.

Those were pleasant hours for Brian, for the sea was fair and he had naught to do but sit with the Bird Daughter. He found himself drawn ever closer to her, admiring her wit and fairness as he did, and he fancied that she was by no means unwilling to talk with him and open her mind as she did to few men. Yet he remembered that he was no more than her vassal, a landless man in truth.

That night the two caracks separated, standing well off the land and keeping good watch, but no sign did they catch of the O'Donnell pirates. Toward morning a stiff wind came upon them from the west, and Brian's men, being all landsmen, got no great joy out of that cruise.

"This wind is like to hold," said Nuala, laughing as she stood on the poop with Brian that morning and watched the decks. "I am afraid that we might as well give over this attempt, Brian. Your men will be in no shape to fight. What think you?"

"Right," nodded Brian slowly, for he saw that those men of his were worse than useless with their sickness.

So they turned about and drove before the wind, but before ever they had got past Slyne Head the men aloft descried a sail to the south that seemed like a large galley. Nuala signaled the other carack to bear down with her, and presently they made out that it was a large sailing galley, which headed straight for them.

"That is none of my ships," exclaimed Nuala, watching. "It seems strange that she does not flee before us, Brian. She bears no ensign, yet she must be from these parts, and would naturally have some fear of pirates."

Brian looked at her rather than the ship, and thought her a fine picture, with her body swinging a little to the sway of the deck and the wind blowing her red cloak around her. The galley came straight for them as if seeking speech, however, and when a falconet was fired from the carack without charge, she lowered her sail and put out her sweeps, coming straight for them.

Nuala sped a word to her sailing-master, and the men let down the sails with shouting and great creaking of ropes. The

Bird Daughter stood under the high poop bulwark, and now she turned to Brian.

"Do you speak with them and find their business, for it seems to me that all is not as it should be, and they would likely know me too well."

Brian nodded, and when the galley had come under their lee he saw that she was well laden, and had for crew a dozen rough-looking men. One of these replied to his hail.

"We are come from Galway, lord, with a gift of stores and wines from O'Donnell Dubh to certain friends of his whom we came to meet. Are you those friends, as we think?"

Brian started in surprise, but needed no word from Nuala. He saw that the Dark Master must have sent this galley out to meet the Millhaven men, and that the crew had taken the two caracks for those pirate ships.

"We are the O'Donnells from Millhaven," he shouted, and ordered the seaman to cast down ropes to the galley. Her master, a stout man with bushy black beard, waved a hand in reply, and after another moment the two craft ground together. The master of the galley got aboard over the low waist of the carack, and Brian ordered a dozen of his own green-faced men down into the smaller ship. At this the galley's master stared somewhat, but came up to the poop.

"Lord, O'Donnell sends you these stores with a message. I am Con Teague of Galway."

"Let us have it," ordered Brian, liking the looks of the man not at all.

"He bade us say that he was leaving Galway to-morrow at dawn with a force of men, and that you should meet him at Bertragh Castle and fall on that place to take it."

"That is good," laughed Brian. "Now learn that you have found the wrong ships, my man. We are not the Millhaven pirates, but I am Brian Buidh, who holds Bertragh; and here is the Lady Nuala, for whom I hold it."

At that Nuala came forward, and Teague looked greatly

astonished, as well he might, and all the Bird Daughter's men fell roaring with laughter. But he could make no resistance, and stood chapfallen while Brian talked with Nuala.

"I must back to the Castle," he said, "and see if this news be true. Do you go on to Gorumna with my men, and I will let loose a pigeon to you. If the Dark Master is indeed on the way, then come with all the men you can spare, and it will go hard if we do not best his royalists, and the pirates later when the latter come."

This was clearly the best plan, so Brian sent Teague down into the galley and followed him, as the light ship was faster than the caracks. Replacing half of Teague's men with O'Malleys, he had the ropes cast off, waved his hand at Nuala, and they drove to the eastward and Bertragh Castle.

Teague made so much moan over losing his ship that Brian promised it back to him when they had reached the castle; the stores and wine, however, he accounted good spoils of war. This put the seaman in better mood, and by noon the fast galley had covered the twenty miles to Bertragh, and cast down her anchor in the little bay beyond the castle, that same bay where Brian had come to grief through O'Donnell's sorcery.

The men crowded down to meet him joyfully, and Brian found that Cathbarr had come home safe with his beeves and was hungry for fight. No sign had been heard of the Dark Master along the roads, however, so Brian set Turlough in charge of getting the stores and wine-casks off the galley, and fell to work putting the castle in shape for defense.

Since there was no need of loosing a pigeon until word came that the Dark Master was actually on the way, he sent out men to have a beacon built on the hills at the bay's head as soon as the enemy was sighted. What with seeing that the bastards and other shot were cleaned and loaded, and stationing his hundred men to the best advantage, he found that the afternoon soon wore away.

"Those are good wines," said Turlough when they sat at meat

that evening, the men eating below in the courtyard around fires. "But I do not like that ship-master."

So far Brian had said nothing of how the galley had been taken, save that they had chanced on it at sea and had heard from Teague that the Dark Master might be on them in another day. As for the O'Malleys, they kept to themselves and talked not at all, so that neither Turlough nor Cathbarr had heard the way of that capture.

"Is she unladen?" asked Brian.

"All save a few barrels. That ship-master was so eager to be off," grunted old Turlough spitefully, "that I stayed the work and put a guard on the galley until morning."

"Give the men a cask of the best wine," ordered Brian shortly.

Having taken upon himself the duties of seneschal, Turlough departed grumbling. While he was gone, Brian's tongue was a little loosened with wine, so that he told Cathbarr of how he had taken the galley, at which the giant bellowed with laughter. Presently from the courtyard came shouting and singing, and Turlough appeared with a beaker of wine.

"The men like it well enough," he said, "yet to me it seems soured. Taste it, Brian; if it be so, then you have made a poor haul on that cruise."

Brian sipped the wine, and in truth it seemed to have soured. Cathbarr made little of that, and would have drunken it except that his clumsy hand knocked it from the table and emptied it all. But as it happened, that mischance saved his life.

A little after, Brian pulled out a Spanish pipe he had got that day from one of the O'Malleys, with some tobacco, and began puffing in great good-humor, for it was long since he had tasted tobacco. Cathbarr watched in awe, never having seen this done before, so that Brian and Turlough had great fun with him. All his life the giant had lived in the mountains and he knew no more than his ax had taught him; though he had seen men smoke before, he had ever accounted it sorcery of some kind, nor could Brian get him to as much as touch the pipe with his finger.

Brian was sorry that the wine had proved sour; the butts were huge ones, and he had counted on their lasting him and his men all the winter through. However, he dismissed the matter from his mind and fell to talking with Turlough and Cathbarr over their arrangements in case of an attack. In the midst, one of the men who had been watching from the tower ran in to say that he had caught sight of a beacon on the hills, which meant that the arch-enemy was on the road.

"Good!" exclaimed Brian, springing up. "Turlough, go fetch me that cage of pigeons. Cathbarr, see that the men are set on the walls—"

He had got no further than this when there came a strange noise from the doorway. Turning, he saw a man staggering forward, choking as he came, and recognized him as one of the Bird Daughter's seamen. The fellow held a bloody sword in his hand.

"What's this?" cried Brian angrily, noting that there was silence upon the court-yard. "Has there been wrangling again—"

"Death!" coughed the O'Malley, staring at him with starting, terrible eyes. "Con Teague—I slew him—too—too late—"

"Man, what is forward?" Brian leaped out and caught the seaman in his arms, for the fellow's head was rolling on his shoulders.

"Death!" whispered the man again. "They are—all dead—"

His head fell back in death, and the sword fell from his hand with a clatter. But from Cathbarr, who had gone to the doorway, came one terrible shout of grief and rage.

"Brian! Our men lie dead—"

"I think the Dark Master has sent us a kindly gift," quoth Turlough Wolf, as Brian rose with horror in his face and let the seaman's body fall. "Now I know why that wine was sour, master!"

CHAPTER XVIII

BRIAN YIELDS BERTRAGH

"**I** DARE NOT trust birds alone in this strait, Cathbarr. Go to that galley with the two O'Malleys and hasten to Gorumna. Bid the Bird Daughter stay and wait further word from me; but take those hundred men of mine with her galleys, and hasten back. If the beacon on the tower is burning, I will be here; if not, and if I can make terms, I will meet you at that tower of yours. Now hasten!"

"But—"

"For God's love go, or my heart will burst!"

Brian sank down on the horse-stone with a groan, and Cathbarr, catching up his ax, fled through the open gates and was gone into the night. Brian gazed up after him, and on the hills he saw that dim beacon-fire heralding the Dark Master.

The six men guarding the galley, two of them being O'Malleys, and three men who had watched on the tower, were all that remained alive in Bertragh besides Turlough and Brian. The men had drunk deep of that poisoned wine; when Con Teague and his men tried to get away after a few had died, they were slain. But so swift was the poison that only one of the O'Malleys had lived to reach Brian.

The fires still burned brightly, and before some of them meat was burning. Sitting in blank despair on a horse-block, Brian saw the dead bodies of a few less than a hundred men lying there. Turlough Wolf and his six gave over trying to put life into any of them, and now the old man came and put his hand on Brian's shoulder.

"Where has Cathbarr of the Ax gone, master?"

Brian told him dully, and Turlough nodded approval, having at length learned all the story of how that galley had been taken.

"Master, there was deep cunning in this. O'Donnell sent that galley to you, or, rather, to the Bird Daughter, and he had spies watching. Had the Gorumna men drunk of that brew, he would have fallen on there; but here came the galley, and now he comes over the hills. And we are few to meet him."

"We will be more when the men come in from the hill-roads before him," and Brian rose up with heavy heart, forcing himself to the task. "Send out a man to haste them in and to warn what men there be at the farms. Also let him send a wagon or two, that these dead may be carried out before the Dark Master falls on us. Send two men to the tower to build a beacon, for Cathbarr will not be back before to-morrow night."

Brian went to the stables where the three carrier-pigeons were caged, and fetched the cage to the great hall. Here he wrote what had happened, with his plan, in small space, fastened it under the wing of a bird, and let loose the pigeon from the courtyard.

Stunned though he was by the sudden and terrible blow, Brian had seized on the only course left him. If he could make shift to hold the castle at all, he would do so; if not, he must make terms and get off to Gorumna that he might take vengeance for this dastardly stroke that had been dealt him.

Nuala had nigh three hundred men in her castle, and he felt that all was not yet lost, even should he have to yield Bertragh. The Dark Master would hardly have a large force with him, and he would know nothing of those hundred men Brian had loaned Nuala; so Brian reckoned that if he could get away, O'Donnell would think him a broken man who could do no further against him.

"Well, that's looking too far ahead," thought Brian very

wearily. "Perchance I am broken, indeed, since I have lost two hundred and a half of men without gain."

An hour later rode in a score of men with wagons, and fell to work getting the dead out of the castle, though for burying there was no time. This score, and two more who came in later, were all the men left to Brian; they reported that the Dark Master would be on them by daybreak, with two hundred Scots troopers and one horse cannon.

"His friends proved niggardly, then," laughed Brian drearily. "We have but to hold the place till to-morrow night, friends, and the O'Malleys will relieve us. Now, one man to watch and the rest of us to rest, for there is work ahead."

Brian, indeed, got some sleep that night, but it was shot through with visions of those poisoned men of his, and their twisted faces gibbered at him, and he thought they shrieked and howled for revenge. When he was roused at dawn, he found the meaning of those noises, since a great storm was sweeping down out of the west, and the farther wore the day, the worse grew the storm.

"Is Heaven itself fighting against us?" he thought bitterly, watching the sea from the battlements. "Against this blast Nuala cannot reach me, if she will."

He got little time to brood, however. Before he had broken his fast the Dark Master's horsemen came in sight—two hundred braw Scots, with wagons and a cannon following after. It was no large force, but Brian found afterward that it was the best the Dark Master could get, since the Galway Irish cared nothing whether the Scots lived or died.

They halted and spread out, half a mile from the castle, and Brian saw that the men were being quartered on the farms round about. Bitterly he wished that he had his lost men, for with them he could have sent those Scots flying home again; but now he was helpless.

With the gates shut and the bastards loaded with bullets to sweep the approach, Brian sent his twenty men to the battlements and watched, with Turlough beside him. It was plain that no offensive operations were under way as yet, and an hour passed quietly; then ten men rode down to the castle under a white flag, and foremost of them was the Dark Master.

"Now, if I were in your place, master," said Turlough, slanting his eyes up at Brian in his shrewd way, "I would loose those bastards and sweep the road bare."

"You are not in my place," said Brian, and the Wolf held his peace.

The Dark Master looked at those bodies piled between the castle and the shore, and it was easy to see that he was laughing and pointing them out to the Scots. At that Brian heard his men mutter no little, and he himself clenched his nails into his palms and cursed bitterly; but he forbade his men to fire and they durst not disobey him. The party rode up under the walls, and the Dark Master grinned at Brian standing above.

"You have great drunkards, Yellow Brian," he called mockingly. "Have all your men drunk themselves to death?"

Brian answered him not, but fingered his hilt; even at that distance the Dark Master seemed to feel the icy blue eyes upon him, for his leer vanished.

"Yield to us, Yellow Brian," he continued, shooting up his head from betwixt his shoulders. "I do not think you have many men in that castle."

"I have enough to hold you till more come," answered Brian.

"Mayhap, and mayhap not," and O'Donnell laughed again. "Keep a watch to seaward, Yellow Brian, and when you see four sail turning the headland, judge if those two caracks of the Bird Daughter's are like to help you."

"If you have no more to say, get you gone," said Brian, feeling the anger in him rising beyond endurance. The Dark Master looked along the walls for a moment, then signed to his men, and they rode off through the driving snow again.

Turlough looked at Brian and Brian at him, and the same thought was in the minds of both. If those Millhaven men had four ships driving down before that storm, as seemed probable enough, the Bird Daughter's two little caracks would never land men under the guns of Bertragh.

About noon the snow fell less thickly, though the storm had risen to great power, and Brian made out that the Scots were bringing forward that cannon of theirs. Having some little knowledge of artillery himself, he drew the charge of bullets from a bastard and put in more powder, then put the bullets back, a full bag of them. He did the same with two more of the bastards on that wall, and when the Scots had halted aimed all three very carefully, and set men by them to fire at his order. The Scots were turning their cannon about, a score of men being in their party, and Brian judged that they were eight hundred paces away—just within range of his bastards.

"The Dark Master lost this hold because he had too many men," he said to Turlough, "and we shall lose it because we have too few; but we will make better use of these shot than did he. Fire, men!"

The three men brought down their linstocks and ran for it, having seen that extra charge of powder set in the cannon. But none of the pieces burst, though they roared loud enough and leaped at their recoil-ropes like mad things. When the white smoke shredded down the wind, Brian's men yelled in great delight, for those Scots and horses about the cannon were stricken down or fleeing, and the piece had not yet been loaded.

"They will get little joy of that cannon," said Brian grimly, and went in to meat.

During the rest of the day the cannon stood there silent, dead horses and men around it; nor was any further attack made. Brian knew well that having found him prepared, the Dark Master would now attack at night and hard did Brian pray that the storm might abate from the west, or at least shift around, so that Nuala's ships could come to his aid.

Instead, the gale only swooped down the wilder, and seemed like to hold a day or more, as indeed it did. About mid-afternoon Turlough came and beckoned him silently out to the rear or seaward battlement and pointed out.

No words passed between the two men, nor were any needed; beating around the southern headland were four flecks of white that Brian knew for ships coming from the west with the storm, and he saw that for once the Dark Master had told the truth.

"I have some skill at war," he said to Turlough that afternoon when they had seen the four ships weather past them and anchor a mile up the bay; "and since the Dark Master's troopers are also skilled at that game, they will fall to work without waste of time or men. We may look to have the dry moat filled with fascines to-night and our gates blown in with petards. At the worst, we can hold that tower, where the powder is stored."

If he had had more men, Brian would have slung the bastards down from the high walls and set them in the courtyard where they could sweep the gates when these had been blown in. But they weighed a ton and half each, and there was no time to build shears to let them down, even had they had spars and ropes at hand. So Brian set them to cover the approach, and had the smaller falcons brought down to the courtyard, all five, where he trained them on the gates and loaded them with bullets heavily.

"Turlough and I will fire these ourselves," he told his men that evening as they made supper together, the men looking forward to the night's work with great joy. "Do the rest of you gather on either hand by the stables, with spare muskets and pistols."

So this was done as he said. Because of the storm Brian did not light his beacon after all, but he stocked the tower with food and wine, and told his men to get there, if they could, when the rest was taken. That tower had Brian's chamber in the lower part and a ladder in the upper part, where was great store of powder.

The five falcons were set in front of the hall doorway, where once Brian had come near to being nailed. Brian loosed another of the pigeons, telling Nuala how things chanced, and of the four pirate ships, and set the last bird in the tower in case of need, which proved a lucky thing for him in the end.

Brian and his men slept after meat, while Turlough Wolf remained watching. It was wearing well on to midnight when the old man woke them all, and Brian went to the walls to hear a thud of hoofs and a murmur of men coming across the wind to him. He sent off men to loose the loaded guns on the outer walls at random, and then suddenly flung lighted cressets over the gates.

A wild yell answered this, and bullets from the men who were filling the dry moat, while others scrambled across it and charged up to the gates with small powder-kegs and petards ready. This was not done without scathe, however; Brian's men loosed their muskets, and one by one the heavy bastards thundered out across the snow, though the result was hard to see in the darkness.

There came a ragged flash of musketry in reply, and that abandoned cannon roared out lustily, though its ball passed far overhead. Brian stood on a demi-bastion that half flanked the gates, and after firing his pistol into the men below, he leaped down the steps into the courtyard and joined Turlough behind the falcons.

"One at a time, Turlough. They'll have the gates down in a minute."

While he waited for the storm to fall, Brian saw that two or three of his men had been hit. He wondered dully that the Dark Master had not made a general assault, and concluded that he must wish to save men. It was a long moment that dragged down on him; then a splash of light burst up, the gates were driven inward and shattered, and with a great roar there fell a rain of riven beams and stones and dirt.

Sheltering in the hall doorway, Brian and Turlough stayed unmoving through an instant of black silence. Out of it broke a wild Scots yell, and in the light of the courtyard cressets a wave of men surged up in the breach. Brian's linstock fell on a falcon, and the little gun barked a hail of bullets across the Scots;

Turlough's gun followed suit, and the first lines of men went down in a struggling mass.

The Dark Master was not to be beaten this time, however. Another wave of Scots swept up, with a mass of men behind them. While some of Brian's men tried to get the two falcons reloaded, a storm of bullets swept across the courtyard, and Brian saw Turlough turn and run for it through the doorway, while two of the men fell over a falcon.

But as the first line of men broke into the courtyard, Brian fired the remaining three cannon as fast as he could touch linstock to powder. The bullet-hail tore the front ranks to shreds, but through the darkling smoke-cloud he saw other men come leaping, and knew that the game was up.

On the next instant his men had closed around him, muskets were stabbing the powder-smoke, and Brian fell to work with his Spanish blade. O'Donnells and Scots together heaved up against them, but Brian's point weaved out between cutlas and claymore and bit out men's lives until the mass of men surged back again like the backleash of a wave that comes against a wall.

Brian heard the Dark Master's voice from somewhere, and with that muskets spat from the gloom and bullets thudded around him. One slapped his steel cap away and another nicked his ear, and a third came so close across his eyes that he felt the hot breath of it; but his men fared in worse case than that, for they were clutching and reeling and fallen, and Brian leaped across the last of them into the hall with bullets driving at his back-piece.

As he ran through the hall he knew that his falcons had punished O'Donnell's men heavily, and that his twenty men had not fallen without some payment for their lives. None the less, Bertragh Castle was now lost to him and to the Bird Daughter; but he thought it likely that he would yet make a play that might nip O'Donnell in the midst of his success.

In this Brian was a true O'Neill and the true luck of the Red Hand had seemed to dog him, for he had lost all his men without suffering a defeat, and now that he was beaten down, he was planning to strike heaviest.

He gained the tower well enough, and found Turlough there to receive him, with food and wine and loaded pistols. They soon had the door of the lower chamber fast barred and clamped, and Brian flung himself down on his bed, panting, but unwounded to speak of.

"Now sleep, master," said the old man. "They will search elsewhere, and finding this door closed will do naught here until the morning."

Brian laughed a little.

"It is not easy to sleep after fighting, Turlough. I think that now I will send off that last pigeon, so give me that quill yonder."

With great care Brian wrote his message, telling what had passed, and saying that he hoped to ride free from the castle next morning. In that case he would be at Cathbarr's tower before evening came, and he told Nuala to have all her men landed there at once, since she could hope to do nothing by sea against the pirate ships.

When the writing was bound to the pigeon's wing he loosed the bird through the seaward casement, and bade Turlough blow out their flickering oil-light.

After eating and drinking a little, they lay down to sleep. Men came and pounded at the door, then departed growling; but Turlough had guessed aright. The Dark Master was plainly speeding the search for Brian elsewhere, and since there was no sign of life from the powder-tower, he did not molest this until close to dawn. Then Brian was wakened by a shock at the door, and he heard the Dark Master's voice outside directing his men. Still he seemed to have no thought that Brian was there, but wanted to get at the powder and into his own chamber again.

Brian took up his pistols and went to a loophole opening on the battlements, while Turlough still crouched on the bed in no little fear. Finding that the Dark Master stood out of his sight,

Brian fired at two of the men under the door, and they fell; then he raised his voice above the shouting that came from outside.

"O'Donnell, are you there?"

The uproar died away, and the other's voice came to him.

"So you are trapped at last, Brian Buidh! Now yield and I promise you a swift hanging."

"Not I," laughed Brian curtly. "There is no lack of powder here, O'Donnell Dubh, and one of my men holds a pistol ready for it."

At this he glanced at Turlough, who grimaced. But from outside came a sudden yell of alarm, and Brian saw a few flee-ing figures, while O'Donnell shouted at his men in furious rage. Brian called out to him again:

"Give me a horse and let me go free with the one man left me, or else I will blow up both tower and castle, and you will have little gain for my death."

"Would you trust my word in this?" cried the Dark Master. Brian smiled.

"Yes, as you must trust mine to leave no fuse in the powder when I am gone."

Then fell silence. Brian hated O'Donnell, as he knew he was hated in return; and so great was the hatred between them that he felt instinctively he could trust the Dark Master to send him out free. It seemed to him that the other would sooner have him go broken and crushed than do him to death, for that would be a greater revenge. Moreover, the Dark Master could know nothing of those men at Gorumna and would have little fear of the Bird Daughter.

And it befell exactly as Brian thought.

"I agree," cried the Dark Master, stepping out in the dawn-light boldly. "You shall go forth empty as you came, Yellow Brian. What of those two-score men you owe me?"

"The time is not yet up," returned Brian, beginning to unbar the door, and he laughed at the mocking voice.

CHAPTER XIX

BRIAN MEETS THE BLACK WOMAN

"THE STORM is over, master, or will be by this night."

"Too late now, Turlough."

Brian and the old man stood in the courtyard, while the Dark Master was seeing to horses being made ready for them. Drawing his cloak farther about his hunched shoulders, the latter turned to Brian with a mocking sneer.

"Now farewell, Brian Buidh, and forget not to repay that loan, if you can gather enough men together. When you come again, you will find me here. A merry riding to you. *Beannacht leath!*"

Brian looked at him grimly.

"Your curse would make better company than your blessing, O'Donnell," he said, and turned to his horse with no more words.

The Scots who were standing around gave vent to a murmur of approval, and Brian saw the black looks passing between them and the wild O'Donnells. The Highlanders had done murdering enough in Ireland since Hamilton brought them over, but they were outspoken men, who had little love for poisoners; and as Brian settled into the saddle with his huge sword slung across his back, he caught more than one word of muttered approval, which the Dark Master was powerless to check.

So Yellow Brian rode out from the castle he had lost, with Turlough Wolf at his heels, and his heart was very sore. Once across the filled-in moat and he saw fifty men at work by the

173

shore, loading the dead into boats to be buried in the bay, for the ground was hard-frozen.

Parties of Scots troopers and the horseless O'Donnells were scattered over the farmlands and country ahead, but these offered no menace as the two horsemen rode slowly through them. For all his bitterness, Brian noted that the four pirate ships had been brought around into the bay before the castle, into which the Scots had moved, while a great number of the O'Donnells had landed and were hastily throwing up brush huts on the height above the shore, evidently intending to camp there for the present.

That was a dark leave-taking for Brian, since he had lost so many men and his castle to boot. Yet more than once he looked back on Bertragh, and when they came to the last rise of ground before the track wound into the hills and woods, he drew rein and pointed back with a curt laugh.

"This night I shall return, Turlough, and I think we shall catch the Dark Master off his guard at last. If we throw part of our men on that camp at dawn and the rest upon the castle, the tables may yet be turned."

"A good rede, Brian O'Neill," nodded the old Wolf approvingly. At thus hearing his name Brian flung Turlough one lightning-swift glance, then pulled out his Spanish sword and threw it high, and caught it again with a great shout.

"Tyr-owen! *Slainte!*"

With that he put spurs to his horse and rode on with better heart, striving to forget his troubles in thinking of the stroke he would deal that night. If those three pigeons had won clear to Gorumna, he would find Nuala and her men waiting at Cathbarr's tower, and before the dawn they would be back again and over the hills.

So they rode onward, and presently came to a stretch of forest, dark against the snow. Suddenly Turlough drew up with a frightened glance around.

"Master—what is that wail? If I ever heard a banshee, that is the cry! Beware of the Little People, master—"

"Nonsense!" exclaimed Brian, drawing rein also and listening. He heard a faint, sobbing cry come from ahead, and so mournful was it, so charged with wild grief, that for an instant his heart stood still, and the color fled from his face.

"It is some woman wailing her dead, Turlough," he said at length, although doubtfully. "Yet I have never heard a *caoine* like it; but onward, and let us see."

"Wait, master!" implored the old man. "Let us cut over the hills and go by another path—"

"Go, if you are afraid," returned Brian, and spurred forward. The other hesitated, but followed unwillingly, and a moment later Brian came upon the cause of that mournful wailing, as the trees closed about them and the road wound into a hollow.

The dingle was so sheltered by the brooding pines that there was little snow, except on the track itself, and no wind. Under the spreading splay-boughs to the right was what seemed to be a heap of rags and tatters, though the wailing cry ceased as the two riders clattered down, with Turlough keeping well behind Brian.

The latter drew rein, seeing that the creature under the pine-boughs was some old crone whose grief seemed more bitter still than his own.

"What is wrong, mother?" he cried cheerily. "Are you from one of the Bertragh farms?"

The tattered heap moved slightly, and a wrinkled, withered face peered up at him.

"Nay, I come from farther than that," and to his surprise there was a mocking note in her voice, though it was weak. "That is a good horse of yours, *ma boucal;* he must trot sixteen miles to the hour, eh?"

"All of that, mother," returned Brian, wondering if the old crone was out of her senses. "Was it you whom I heard wailing a moment ago? Where is your home?"

The old woman broke into a cackle of hideous laughter.

"My home, is it? Once I had a home, Yellow Brian—and it was in Dungannon, with Tyr-owen and Cormac and Art and the noblest of the chiefs of Ulster to do me honor! Have you forgotten me, Brian O'Neill, since we met at the Dee Water?"

Then Brian gave a great cry, and swung down to earth, for now he recognized the Black Woman. But as he strode toward her she tried to rise and failed, and forth from the midst of her rags came a quick gush of red blood. Brian leaped forward and caught her in his arms, pitying her.

"I knew you," she gasped out weakly, clutching at his shoulder. "I knew you, son of Tyr-owen! You had yellow hair, but your face was the face I once loved, the face of the great Hugh—"

She stopped abruptly, and her words were lost in a choking gasp as blood came from her mouth. Brian swore.

"Mile Mollaght! What has happened here, woman? Are you wounded?"

"Aye, those dogs of O'Donnells," she moaned feebly. Then new strength came to her, and she peered up with another cackle. "But did I not tell wisely, son? Have you not found Cathbarr of the Ax and the Bird Daughter even as I foretold?"

"Yes, yes," returned Brian impatiently. "Where are you wounded, mother? We can take you—"

"Peace, avic," she cried. "They came on me last night, and my life is gone. You shall take vengeance for the old *calliagh*, Brian—but first I must talk. Do you know who I am, avic—or who I was, rather?"

"How should I know that, mother?" answered Brian. "Old Turlough Wolf, yonder, swears you are some witch—"

"Turlough!" The hag raised herself on his arm, cackling. "So the old Wolf is still living! Do *you* know me, Turlough? Do you remember the sorrowful day of the earl's flight?"

Old Turlough, who had ridden closer, bent over and looked down, fear in his face. Suddenly he straightened up again with a wild cry.

"Noreen of Breffny! By my hand, it is the earl's love!"

"Aye, the earl's love!" she gasped out, falling back. "I was his love in truth, Yellow Brian, and he loved me above all the rest, though another's hand closed his eyes and laid him to earth in Rome. I knew you would come, Brian—I saw you at Drogheda, though you saw me not, and I bade you come here into the West, and I have watched over you—"

She coughed horribly, clutching at Brian's arm. He stared down at her in amazement, for the incredible story seemed true enough. This old hag had been that Noreen of Breffny of whom he had heard much—the fairest maid of the North, whom the great earl had loved to the last, though the church had not blessed their union.

Brian's old Irish nurse had often told him of the "Breffny lily," and it was bitter and hard to realize that this ancient hag, withered and shrunk and done to death by the Dark Master's men, had been the fairest maid in Ulster. She gasped out a little more of her story, and Brian found that his wild surmises had been true; after seeing him and recognizing him for one of the earl's house, she had instantly led his mind to this part of the country, being aware of the strife between O'Donnell and Nuala O'Malley. It had been a crazed notion enough, and since then she had kept as near to him as possible in the half-sane idea that she might help him.

How she had managed to do it ever remained a mystery to Brian, since his marches had been none of the slowest, but she had done so.

"Where are—your men?" she exclaimed after a little. Brian told her what had chanced at the castle, and she broke out in a last wild cackling laugh.

"Tyr-owen's luck!" she cried. "Betrayed and blasted, betrayed and blasted—but the root of the tree is still strong, Yellow Brian—give me your blessing, master—give Noreen your blessing before you go to Rome, Hugh *mo mhuirnin*—"

Brian's face blanched and his hands trembled, for he saw that her wandering mind took him for his grandsire.

"Dhia agus mhuire orth," he murmured, and with a little sob the Black Woman died.

Silence fell upon the dingle, as Brian gazed down at the woman his grandfather had loved, and whose love had been no less. Then Turlough pushed his horse closer, looking down with a shrewd leer.

"Said she not that it would be a black day when you met her again, master?" he queried with awe in his voice. "I think—"

"Keep silence!" commanded Brian shortly. "Get down from that horse and dig a grave."

"But the ground is frozen—" began old Turlough in dismay. Brian gave him one look, and the old man hastily dismounted, crossing himself and mumbling.

Brian joined him, and they managed to scoop out a shallow grave with knife and sword, laid the old woman in it, and covered her up again. It was a sorry burial for the love of the great earl, but it was the best they could do.

Shaken more than he cared to admit, Brian mounted and rode on in silence. As he had thought, there was nothing supernatural about this weird Black Woman, except, perhaps, the manner in which she had contrived to keep close to him. She had warned him at the Stone Mountain, and she must have been keeping close to Bertragh ever since, unseen by any, with her unhinged mind driving her forward relentlessly.

"Poor woman!" he thought darkly, gazing into the hills ahead. "There has been little luck to any who ever followed an O'Neill or loved an O'Neill! And now it seems likely that the same ill luck of all my family is to dog my heels, bringing me up to the heights, only to cast me down lower than before. Well, I may fall, but it shall not be until I have dragged down the Dark Master. If I fall not I may yet best the ill-luck and conquer Millhaven for my own."

With that his mind leaped ahead again as the plan outlined itself to him. The O'Donnell pirates must have brought their whole force to the Dark Master's aid, and if he could but cut off that camp of theirs between the castle and the shore, Nuala O'Malley might bring her two ships against the weakened four and take them all.

Then, when the castle had fallen, he could sail north to Millhaven, reduce the stronghold there, and let fly his own banner at last. It was a good plan, but it hung on many things.

With a short laugh at his own fancies he turned in the saddle as the voice of Turlough broke into his musings.

"I mind the last time I saw the poor woman back yonder, master. It was just before the great flight, and I mind now that she was not so ill-looking even then, though she was well past her youth, and that was forty years ago. Tyr-connall's bag-pipe men were blowing as we marched to Lough Swilly, and two earls rode in front when the poor *caillin* rushed out and flung herself under Tyr-owen's horse—oh, *Mhuire as truagh, Mhuire as truagh* for the old days! And when the earl died, her name was on his lips, and I came home again to find her disappeared. Oh, what sorrow for the old days! Would that I had died in Rome with the princes—"

"Stop that wailing," interrupted Brian sternly, for the old man was lashing himself into a frenzy of grief. "Put spurs to that horse of yours, Turlough, for we must reach Cathbarr's tower by noon if possible in order to start the men off over the hills. It'll be a long night's march, and I've no time to be idling here on the road."

Upon which he dug in his spurs and urged his steed into a gallop, and in order to keep up, Turlough Wolf had to give over his laments and do likewise. Brian forced himself to bend all his energies toward carrying out his final desperate plan, but he silently vowed that the old woman who had so foully been cut down by the O'Donnells should not die unavenged.

On they galloped without pause, gained the head of Bertraghboy Bay, and swung to the east on the last stretch of the trip. The storm which had arisen so inopportunely was now dying away, and the sun was breaking through the gray clouds; when they turned out from the main track into the hill-paths that led to Cathbarr's tower, the rough ground made them slow their pace. When they were still three miles from the tower, however, Brian gave a shout.

"Men, Turlough! Cathbarr has sent out men to meet us!"

So, indeed, it proved, and five minutes later a dozen men met them with yells of delighted welcome. From these overjoyed fellows Brian quickly learned that Cathbarr was at the tower and that Nuala O'Malley had just arrived there.

So, leaving them to follow, he and Turlough went on at their best speed, and twenty minutes later they topped that same long rise from which Brian had first gazed down on the little promontory where stood Cathbarr's tower. But now, as he saw what lay beneath, he drew up with a shout of amazement.

For around the tower and at the base at the neck of land were camped a goodly force of men, while at anchor near the tower lay—not Nuala's two ships alone, but also those other two of her kinsmen!

"Those two O'Malleys have returned from the south," exclaimed Turlough in wild delight. "That means more men and ships, master—we will cut off those Millhaven pirates to a man!"

Brian sent out a long shout, but his arrival had already been noted. As he rode down the slope, men poured from the camp and tower, and ahead of them all came Cathbarr of the Ax, with Nuala and Lame Art and Shaun the Little behind him.

"Welcome!" bellowed the giant with a huge laugh, pulling Brian from his horse with a great hug of delight. "Welcome, brother!"

Brian escaped from his grip and bowed over the Bird Daughter's hand. As he rose, he saw that her face had lost its ruddy hue, and that her eyes were ringed with darkness. Before he could speak she smiled and gripped his hand.

"The birds came safe, and we know all. Yesterday arrived these kinsmen of mine, and their force is joined to our own, Yellow Brian—"

Brian held up his hand, halting her suddenly, and silence fell on the men who had crowded around. For a moment he gazed into her deep eyes, then flung up his head and his voice rang clear and stern in the stillness.

"Lady Nuala," he said quietly, "I promised you that when I slew the Dark Master I would tell you my name. Before another day has passed I shall have slain him; and now I tell you and your kinsmen that I renounce all fealty to you."

At this the Bird Daughter started, staring in amazement, while an abrupt oath burst from Lame Art. Brian went on calmly.

"This I do because it is not meet that The O'Neill should give fealty to any, Lady Nuala. I am Brian O'Neill, of right The O'Neill and Earl of Tyr-owen, though these are empty titles. And this night you and I shall fall on Bertragh together, Bird Daughter, and when we have won it again it shall be yours as of old."

And amid a great roar of shouts welling up around him Brian bowed to Nuala.

"Then, Brian O'Neill," she said, quieting the tumult a little, "am I to understand that you wish to make pact with me, and to receive no reward?"

For a moment he gazed openly and frankly into her eyes, and under his look the red crept into her cheeks again; yet her own eyes did not flinch.

Brian laughed out.

"Yes, lady! It may be that I shall have a reward to ask of you, but that may not be until I have won back what I have lost for you."

"And what if the reward be too great?"

"Why, that shall be for you to say!" and Brian laughed again. "Is it agreed, Bird Daughter?"

For an instant he thought she meant to refuse, as she drew herself up and met his level eyes; the men around held their breaths, and the O'Malley chiefs glanced at each other in puzzled wonder. Then her quick laugh rippled out and she gave him her hand.

"Agreed, Brian—and I hope that you can shave that yellow beard of yours by to-morrow!"

And the great yell that went up from the men drowned all else in Brian's ears.

CHAPTER XX

THE STORM BURSTS

"NOW, THE first thing is to see what force of men we have," said Brian, after the midday meal. They were all gathered in Cathbarr's tower before a log fire, and were preparing the plan of campaign.

"I have my hundred and eighty men," said Nuala. "When that last pigeon came from you I set out at once. With the hundred men under Cathbarr, we have close to three hundred. You can take them all, for my kinsmen here have enough and to spare to handle my two ships as well as theirs."

"Good!" exclaimed Brian, as the two O'Malleys nodded. "I think that by striking at dawn we shall find most of the O'Donnells ashore or in the castle, and if you time your sailing to strike on their four ships at the same time we may easily take castle, camp, and ships at one blow."

"If all went as men planned we would not need to pray Heaven for aid," quoth Shaun the Little sententiously. Brian glanced at him.

"Eh? What do you mean by that?"

"Nothing," returned the wide-shouldered seaman with a shrug. "Except that there may be more to it than we think, Brian."

"The Dark Master will not suspect your return so suddenly," spoke up Nuala. "Pay no heed to Shaun, Brian—he was ever a croaker. When think you we had best start?"

"I am no seaman," laughed Brian. "Get there at dawn, that is all. I will send on my men at once, then; since we have only two horses, Cathbarr and I will ride after them later and catch them up. Will you take the men, Turlough, or bide here out of danger?"

"I think it will be safest with the Lady Nuala," hesitated the old man craftily.

"Little you know her, then," roared Lame Art, his cousin joining in the laugh.

So Turlough had decided, however, and he stuck to it. Brian then described closely how the four pirate ships lay in the bay under Bertragh, while Shaun went out to arrange the distribution of his men on Nuala's ships.

The arrangements having been perfected, Brian saw his three hundred men troop off on their march over the hills, after which he told Nuala at greater length all that had taken place in the castle since his parting with her at sea. Bitter and unrestrained were the curses of the O'Malleys as they heard of how his men had been poisoned, while Nuala's eyes flamed forth anger.

"There shall be no quarter to these O'Donnells," she cried hotly. "Those whom we take shall hang, and the Scots with them—"

"Not the Scots," exclaimed Brian quickly. "They are honest men enough, Nuala, and may serve us well as recruits. If we find them in the castle, as I think we shall, we may leave them there until we have finished the Millhaven men; however, it is possible that my men will find the castle almost unguarded, and so take it at the first blow. However that turns out, the Dark Master shall not escape us this time."

During the afternoon, when the two O'Malleys were busily getting their ships in order for the coming fray, Brian sat in the tower with Nuala. He told her freely of himself, and although neither of them referred to that reward of which he had spoken at their meeting, Brian knew well that he would claim it.

He did not conceal from himself that the Black Woman had guided him to more than conquest by sword. The Bird Daughter was such a woman as he had dreamed of, but had never found at the Spanish court, and he knew that whether there was love in her heart or not, his own soul was in her keeping.

Perhaps he was not the only one who knew this, for as Lame Art rowed out with his cousin, the latter nodded back at the tower.

"What think you of this ally, Art Bocagh? Could he be truly the Earl's grandson?"

"I know not," grunted the other. "But I do not care whether he be Brian Buidh or Brian O'Neill or Brian the devil—he is such a man as I would fain see sitting in Gorumna Castle, Shaun!"

And Shaun the Little nodded with a grin.

When the sun began its westering, Brian and Cathbarr rode back from the tower with food and weapons at their saddle-bows, and they paused at the hill-crest to watch the four ships weigh anchor and up sail, then went on into the hills. They were to meet their men at that valley where the Dark Master had been defeated and broken in the first siege, and jogged along slowly, resting as they rode.

"Brother," said Cathbarr suddenly, fingering the haft of his ax and looking at Brian, "do you remember my telling you, that night after we had bearded the Dark Master and got the loan of those two-score men, how an old witch-woman had predicted my fate?"

"Yes," returned Brian, with a sharp glance. In the giant's face there was only a simple good-humor, however, mingled with a childlike confidence in all things. "And I told you that you were not bound to my service."

"No, but I am bound to your friendship," laughed Cathbarr rumblingly. "I can well understand how I might die in a cause not mine own, since I am fighting for you; but I cannot see how death is to come upon me through water and fire, brother!"

"Nonsense," smiled Brian. "Death is far from your heels, brother, unless you are seeking it."

"Not I, Brian. I neither seek nor avoid if the time comes. Only I wish that witch-woman had told me a little more—"

"Keep your mind off it, Cathbarr," said Brian. "In Spain the Moriscoes say that the fate of man is written on his forehead, and God is just."

"What the devil do I care about that?" bellowed Cathbarr. "I care not when I die, brother—but I want to strike a blow or two first, and how can that be done if death comes by water and fire?"

"Well, take heart," laughed Brian, seeing the cause of the other's anxiety. "You are not like to die from that cause to-night, and I promise you blows enough and to spare."

Cathbarr grunted and said no more. The last of the storm had fled away, and the two men rode through a glittering sunset and a clear, cold evening that promised well for the morrow.

They traveled easily, and it was hard on midnight when a sentry stopped them half a mile from the hollow where the men were resting. Brian noted with approval that no fires had been lighted, and he and Cathbarr at once lay down to get an hour's sleep among the men.

Two hours before daybreak the camp was astir, and Brian gathered his lieutenants to arrange the attack. Thinking that the Dark Master would be in the castle, he and Cathbarr took a hundred men for that attack, ordering the rest to get as close to the camp as might be, but not to attack until he had struck on the castle, and to cut off the O'Donnells from their ships. Then, assured that the plan was understood, he and Cathbarr loaded their pistols and set out with the hundred.

Brian ordered his men to give quarter to all the Scots who would accept it, if they got inside the castle, and as they marched forward through the darkness he found to his delight that O'Donnell seemed to have no sentries out.

"We have caught the black fox this time," muttered Cathbarr, after they had passed the camp-fires without discovery and the black mass of the castle loomed up ahead. "They will hardly have repaired those gates by now, brother."

Brian nodded, and ordered his men to rest, barely a hundred paces from the castle. Since there was no need of attacking before dawn, in order to let Nuala come up the bay, he went forward with Cathbarr to look at the gates.

These, as nearly as he could tell, were still shattered in; there were fires in the courtyard, and sentries were on the wall, but their watch was lax and the two below were not discovered. They rejoined the hundred, and Brian bade Cathbarr follow him through the hall to that chamber he himself had occupied in the tower, where O'Donnell was most likely to be found.

"Well, no use of delaying further," he said, when at length the grayness of dawn began to dull the starlight. Since to light matches would have meant discovery, he had brought with him those hundred Kerry pikemen Nuala had recruited after the dark Master's defeat, and he passed on the word to follow.

The mass of men gained the moat before a challenge rang out from above, and with that Brian leaped forward at the gates. A musket roared out, and another, but Brian and Cathbarr were in the courtyard before the Scots awakened. A startled group barred their way to the hall, then Brian thrust once, the huge ax crashed down, and they were through.

Other men were sleeping in the hall, but Brian did not stop to battle here, running through before the half-awakened figures sensed what was forward. A great din of clashing steel and yells was rising from the court; then he and Cathbarr gained the seaward battlements and rushed at the Dark Master's chamber. The door was open—it was empty.

For a moment the two stared at each other in blank dismay. With a yell, a half-dozen Scots swirled down on them, but Brian threw up his hand.

"The castle is mine," he shouted. "You shall have quarter!"

The Scots halted, and when two or three of the Kerry pikemen dashed up with news that the rest of the garrison had been cut down or given quarter, they surrendered.

Brian's first question was as to O'Donnell.

"Either at the camp or aboard one of his kinsmen's ships,"

returned one of the prisoners. "They were carousing all last evening."

At the same instant Cathbarr caught Brian's arm and whirled him about.

"Listen, brother!"

So swift had been Brian's attack that the castle had been won in a scant three minutes. Now, as he listened, there came a ragged roar of musketry, pierced by yells, and he knew that the camp was attacked.

With that, a sudden fear came on him that he would again be outwitted. There was a thin mist driving in from the sea which would be dissipated with the daybreak, and if the Dark Master was on one of the ships he might get away before Nuala's caracks could arrive. Brian had been so certain that he would find O'Donnell in the castle that the disappointment was a bitter one, but he knew that there was no time to lose.

"Come," he ordered Cathbarr quickly, "get a score of the men and to the camp. Leave the others here to hold the castle if need be."

As he strode through the courtyard and the sullen groups of Scots prisoners, he directed the Kerry men to load the bastards on the walls and give what help might be in destroying the pirate ships. Then, with Cathbarr and twenty eager men at his back, he set off for the camp at a run, fearful that he might yet be too late.

The day was brightening fast, and from the camp rose a mighty din of shouts and steel and musketry. Brian's men had charged after one hasty volley, but their leader gave a groan of dismay as he saw that instead of attacking from the seaward side as he had ordered, they were pouring into the camp from the land side.

O'Donnell must have landed the greater part of his men, for Brian's force was being held in check, though they had swept in among the brush huts. Over the tumult Brian heard the piercing voice of the Dark Master, and with a flame of rage hot in his mind he sped forward and found himself confronted by a yelling mass of O'Donnells.

Then fell a sterner battle than any Brian had waged. In the lessening obscurity it was hard to tell friend from foe, since the mist was swirling in off the water and holding down the powder-smoke. Brian saved his pistols, and, with Cathbarr at his side, struck into the wild, shaggy-haired northern men; they were armed with ax and sword and skean, and Brian soon found himself hard beset despite the pikemen behind.

The Spanish blade licked in and out like a tongue of steel, and Brian's skill stood him in good stead that morn. Ax and broadsword crashed at him, and as he wore no armor save a steel cap, he more than once gave himself up for lost. But ever his thin, five-foot steel drove home to the mark, and ever Cathbarr's great ax hammered and clove at his side, so that the fight surged back and forth among the huts, as it was surging on the other side where was the Dark Master, holding off the main attack.

Little by little the mist eddied away, however, and the day began to break. A fresh surge of the wild O'Donnells bore down on Brian's party, and as they did so a man rose up from among the wounded and stabbed at Brian with his skean. Brian kicked the arm aside, but slipped in blood and snow and went down; as a yell shrilled up from the pirates, Cathbarr leaped forward over him, swinging his ax mightily. With the blunt end he caught one man full in the face, then drove down his sharp edge and clove another head to waist. For an instant he was unable to get out his ax, but Brian thrust up and drove death to a third, then stood on his feet again.

At the same instant there came a roar from across the camp where his main body of men were engaged, and Brian thrilled to the sound. As he afterward found, it was done by Turlough's cunning word; but up over the din of battle rose the great shout that struck dismay to the pirates and heartened Brian himself to new efforts.

"Tyr-owen! Tyr-owen!"

With a bellow of "Tyr-owen!" Cathbarr went at the foe, and Brian joined him with his own battle-cry on his lips for the first time in his life. The shout swelled louder and louder, and among the huts Brian got a glimpse of the Dark Master. In vain he tried to break through the Millhaven men, however; they stood like a wall, dying as they fought, but giving no ground until the ax and the sword had cloven a way, although the remnant of the twenty pikemen were fighting like fiends.

Suddenly a yell of dismay went up from the O'Donnell ranks, and they broke in wild confusion. Leaning on his sword and panting for breath, Brian looked around and saw what had shattered them so swiftly.

While the stubborn fight had raged, the eastern sky had been streaming and bursting into flame. Now, sharply outlined against the crimson water, appeared Nuala's four ships close on those of the pirates. Even as he looked, Brian saw their cannon spit out white smoke, while from behind came a deeper thunder as the castle's guns sent their heavy balls over the pirate ships.

These were anchored a hundred yards from shore, and Brian saw the danger that betided as the stream of fugitives swept down toward the boats. Nuala's ships were undermanned, for he had counted on cutting off most of the pirates in the camp; should the Dark Master get to the ships with his men, things were like to go hard.

"To the boats!" cried Brian to Cathbarr, and leaping over the dead, the two joined their men and poured down on the shore.

The Dark Master himself stood by one of the boats, and others were filling fast with men as they were shoved down. Brian tried to cut his way to O'Donnell, but before he could do so the Dark Master had leaped aboard and oars were out. Fully aware of their danger, those of the pirates who could do so got into their boats and lay off the shore, while others splashed aboard; Brian led his men down with a rush, cutting down man after man, splashing out into the swirling water and hacking at those in the boats, but all in vain. Some half-dozen of the boats got off, crowded with men, while the remnant of the pirates held off Brian's force that their master might escape.

Drawing out of the fight, Brian pulled forth his pistols and emptied them both at the figure of O'Donnell. He saw the Dark Master reel, and the rower next him plunged forward over the bows, but the next moment O'Donnell had taken up the oar himself and was at work in mad haste. Brian groaned and flung away his pistols.

Those aboard the pirate ships had already cut the cables and were striving to make sail, for there was a light off-shore breeze in their favor, with an ebbing tide. The O'Malley ships were close on them, however, and as the cannon crashed out anew the masts of one O'Donnell ship crashed over. But the Dark Master's boat was alongside another of the ships, whose sails were streaming up, and now his cannon began to answer those of Nuala.

But Brian stood in bitterness, unmindful of the wild yells of his men, for once more the Dark Master had escaped his hand at the last moment. Shaun the Little had been correct in his "croakings."

CHAPTER XXI

CATHBARR YIELDS UP HIS AX

BRIAN GAZED out at the scene before him in dull despair. So close were the ships that he could clearly make out Nuala's figure, with its shimmering mail and red cloak, on the poop of the foremost.

Her second carack had fallen behind, a shot having sent its foremast overside, but the other two ships were driving in. All three were lowering sail, for the Dark Master's craft were unable to get out of the bay and were giving over the attempt; his disabled ship was sending over its men to reinforce him, and Brian saw all his own efforts gone for nothing.

There came a new burst of cannon, and through the veil of smoke he perceived that Nuala was laying her carack alongside one of the pirate ships. But it was not that on which stood the Dark Master; his was the ship closest to the castle, and Lame Art was bearing down on him, while Shaun the Little stood for the third, spitting out a final broadside as he came about and lowered sail.

The crowding men on the shore had fallen silent as they watched the impending conflict, but now Brian felt Cathbarr touch his arm, and turned.

"Why so doleful, brother?" grinned the giant; though blood dripped into his beard from a light slash over the brow, his eyes were as clear and childlike as ever, and the rage of battle had gone from him. "Let us join in that fight, you and I?"

"Eh?" Brian started, staring at him. "How may that be?"

"Ho, here is our captain given way to despair!" bellowed Cathbarr, and his fist smote down on Brian's back. "Wake up, brother!
We have three boats here, and we can still strike a blow or two!"

Now Brian wakened to life indeed. He saw the three boats
on the shore, with dead men hanging over them, and leaped
instantly into action.

"Push out those boats—get the oars, there!" he shouted, leaping down to help shove them out. The men saw his intent, and
sprang to work with a howl of delight.

In no long time the dead were flung out, and the boats pushed
down until they were afloat. Brian leaped into one, Cathbarr
into another, and men piled in after them until the craft were
almost awash.

An eddy in the veil of smoke that hung over the bay showed
Brian that Lame Art's ship had grappled with that of O'Donnell,
and with renewed confidence thrilling in him, he shouted to his
men to get aboard the O'Malley ship. The Bertragh cannon had
ceased to thunder as the ships came together, but from the ships
balls were hailing, musketry was crackling, and the water was
tearing into spurting jets around the boats.

Brian's men fell to their oars in sorry fashion enough, but
they made up in energy what they lacked in skill. Driving past
Nuala's ship, Brian saw that she had also grappled and that the
battle was raging over her bulwarks, but sorely tempted to turn
aside though he was, he waved his men on.

They rowed close under the ship to which she was fastened,
and as they sped past the O'Donnells saw them, and gave them
a scattering volley. One or two of Brian's men went down, and a
cry broke from him as he saw a round shot heaved over into his
third boat, sinking her; then they were past, and bearing down
on Art Bocagh's ship.

"Tyr-owen for O'Malley!"

Cathbarr's bellow rose over the tumult, and his boat crashed
into the waist of the ship just as Brian leaped up into the
mizzen-chains. His feet gained hold on a triced-up port, and

as he looked down he saw a swell heave up the two boats, then bring them down together with a splintering smash.

The result was dire confusion. None of the men were seamen, but some of them gained the side of Brian, others scrambled in through the ports, and more than one of them fell short and went down. Standing in the sinking boat with the water swirling about his ankles, Cathbarr caught up his ax and leaped; a moment later Brian was over the bulwarks with the giant at his side, and the O'Malleys welcomed them with a yell of joy.

They were badly needed, indeed. The Dark Master had led his men in furious onslaught across the waist of the ship, and Art Bocagh was being beaten back to the poop despite his stubborn resistance. Brian saw that the Dark Master's men far outnumbered Art's, while from the rigging of each ship musketeers were sending down bullets into the mêlée. With a shout, Brian and Cathbarr led their men on the O'Donnell flank, and the tide of battle turned.

At the first instant the rush of men bore Brian against the Dark Master, who was fighting like a demon. Brian caught the snarl on the other's pallid face, and struck savagely; O'Donnell parried the blow with his skean and returned it, but Brian warded with his left arm and swept down his blade. The Dark Master flung himself back, but not far enough, and Brian saw the point rip open the pallid cheek. Even as he pressed his advantage, however, another surge of men separated them.

Now Brian gave over every thought save that of reaching his enemy again, and fell on the O'Donnells with stark madness in his face. A pistol roared into his stubbly beard and the ball carried off his steel cap, but he cut down the man and pressed into the midst of the pirates, cutting and thrusting in terrible rage.

At sight of him men bore back; the icy flame in his eyes took the heart from those who faced him, and behind rose Cathbarr's wild bellows as the giant hewed through after Brian. Back went the pirates, and farther back. Brian found that he had cut his way to Lame Art, and with a yell the forces joined and swept on the Dark Master's men.

O'Donnell had vanished, and now his men were swept back to the bulwarks and over to their own deck. Here they made a brief stand; then Cathbarr leaped over into the midst and his ax crushed down two men at once; Brian followed him, and for an instant it seemed that they would sweep all before them.

Just then, however, Lame Art toppled from the bulwarks with a bullet through him from above, and the Dark Master's disappearance was explained by a rain of grenades that whirled among the O'Malleys. They gave back in dismay, Brian and Cathbarr were forced after them, and the Dark Master himself led his men in a mad stream over the bulwarks once more.

There was no stopping them now. The death of Art Bocagh had disheartened his men, and amid flashing steel and spurting fire Brian and Cathbarr retreated to the quarterdeck. Here they had a brief breathing space until the pirates came at them anew, and with such fury that three of them gained a footing to one side. Brian went at them with a shout, thrust one man through the body, sent a second back with his bare fist, and as the third man struck down at him a pikeman transfixed the man before the blow could fall.

The boarders drew back, but as they did so a great heave of the grinding ships broke the hastily flung grapplings. The ships were borne apart, and the Dark Master with most of his men remained in the waist of the O'Malley ship.

This gave a new turn to the conflict. O'Donnell had to master the ship to win free, and when Brian saw this he gave a great laugh and rejoined Cathbarr. A quick glance around showed him that Nuala was slowly winning her grappled decks, while Shaun the Little was hanging off and sending his cannon crashing into the third pirate ship. The two disabled craft were slowly drawing together with the tide, which was forcing all eight into the bay, and were pounding away with their guns as they came.

Now the combat resolved itself into a desperate struggle for possession of the quarterdeck, which Brian and Cathbarr held. The Dark Master's men swarmed up at them bravely enough, but the ax and sword flashed up and down, and time after time the Millhaven men fell back, unable to win a footing. Twice the Dark Master himself led them, snarling with baffled rage, but the first time a pikeman thrust him down and the second time Cathbarr's ax glanced from his helm.

O'Donnell reeled back and was lost to sight for a time.

"That was a poor blow," grunted the giant in disgust. " 'Ware, brother! Stand aside!"

Brian leaped away as the men behind him ran out a falcon and sent its blast into the crowd below in the waist. A dozen men went down under that storm of death, but almost at the same moment a grenade burst behind the falcon, and with that Brian was driven back as a keg of powder tore out half the quarterdeck in a bursting wall of flame and smoke.

Barely had the shattering roar died out when Brian's reeling senses caught a wild yell of dismay from his men.

"Fire! The ship is afire forward!"

Brian saw that the grenades had indeed fired the ship forward, while the explosion had sent the quarterdeck into a burst of fire also, and the lowered but unfurled sails were roaring up in flame.

Up poured the O'Malleys, and Brian staggered back to the poop. He had a vision of the great form of Cathbarr heaving up through the smoke, blackened and bleeding, but with the ax whirling like a leaf and smiting down men; then Brian gained the poop, helped the giant up, and with the few men left they turned to drive down the pirates, who were striving desperately to win the ship before it was too late.

As he stood with Cathbarr at the narrow break of the poop, beating down man after man, Brian knew that it was only a question of time now, for the whole ship was breaking into flame forward. Suddenly he felt a tug at his buff coat, and looked down to see his belt fall away, sundered at his side by a bullet. He thought little of it, for he had half a dozen slight wounds, and turned to smite down at a man who had leaped for the poop; as his sword sheared through helm and skull, there came another tug, and Brian felt a bullet scrape along his ribs.

The O'Donnells drew back momentarily, and in the brief pause Brian saw the figure of the Dark Master by the starboard rail in the waist, aiming up at him with a pistol, while two men behind him were hastily charging others. Cathbarr saw the action also, and hastily flung Brian aside, but too late. A burst of smoke flooded over the waist, and Brian caught the pistol-flash through it, as the ball ripped his left arm from shoulder to elbow. Then the pirates were at the poop again, and the waist was shut out by the flooding smoke as the wind drove it down from forward.

With a scant dozen men behind them, Brian and Cathbarr once more beat the enemy back; the giant swung his ax less lightly now, and seemed to be covered with wounds, though most of them were slight. Brian still eyed the waist for another glimpse of the Dark Master, but the smoke was thick and he could see nothing. In the lull he flung a wan smile at Cathbarr, who stood leaning on his ax, his mail-shirt shredded and bloody.

"Are you getting your fill of battle, brother?"

"Aye," grinned the giant, "and we had best swim for it in another minute or the ship—look! *M'anam an diaoul!* Look!"

At his excited yell Brian turned, as a ball whistled between them. There below, in a boat half full of dead, but with two men at the oars, stood the Dark Master, just lowering his pistol. He flung the empty weapon up at Brian with a hoarse yell of anger, and passed from sight beneath the ship's counter, toward the stern.

Realizing only that his enemy was escaping, Brian whirled and darted for the poop-cabins. He was dimly conscious of a mass of figures behind, amid whom stood Cathbarr with the ax heaving up and down, then he was in the cabins. Jerking open the door to the stern-walk, he saw the Dark Master's boat directly underneath, hardly six feet from him.

"Tyr-owen!" yelled Brian, and dropping his sword, but holding his skean firmly, he hurdled the stern-walk railing and leaped.

At that wild shout the Dark Master looked up, but he was too late. Brian hurtled down, his body striking O'Donnell full in the chest and driving him over on top of the two rowers, so that all four men sprawled out over the dead. For an instant the shock drove the breath out of Brian, then he felt a hand close on his throat, and struck out with his skean.

One of the rowers gurgled and fell back, and Brian rolled over just as steel sank into his side. Giddy and still breathless, he gained his knees to find the Dark Master thrusting at him from the stern, while at his side the other rower was rising. Brian brought up his fist, caught the man full on the chin, and drove him backward over the gunwale. The lurch of the boat flung the Dark Master forward, Brian felt a sickening wrench of pain as the sword pierced his shoulder and tore loose from O'Donnell's hand, then he had clutched his enemy's throat, and his skean went home.

Spent though both men were, the sting of the steel woke the Dark Master to a burst of energy. As the two fell over the thwarts, he twisted above and bore Brian down and tried to break the grip on his throat, but could not. For the second time in his life Brian felt that he had a wild animal in his grasp; the sight of the snarling face, the venomous black eyes, and the consciousness that his own strength was slowly ebbing, all roused him to a last great effort.

The smoke-pall had shut out everything but that wolfish face, and as he writhed up even that seemed to dim and blur before his eyes, so that in desperate fear he struck out again and again, blindly. The blows fell harmless enough, for all his strength was going into that right hand of his; he did not know that his fingers were crushing out the Dark Master's life, that O'Donnell's face was purple and his hands feebly beating the air.

Brian knew only that the terrible face was hidden from him

by some loss of vision, some horrible failure of sight due to his weakness. Suddenly there was a great crash at his side, and he thought that a huge ax with iron twisted around its haft had fallen from the sky and sheared away half the gunnel of the boat. He struck out again with his skean, and felt the blow go home—and with that there came a terrific, blinding roar. The smoke-veil was rent apart by a sheet of flame, Brian realized that the burning ship must have blown up, and then a blast of hot wind drove down against him and smote his senses from him.

CHAPTER XXII

THE STORM OF MEN
COMES TO REST

"**VERY WELL**, Turlough. Tell Captain Peyton that I will give him an answer to his message to-night, then bid my kinsman Shaun entertain him in the hall, with the other officers. Send some food up here, and I may come down later."

"And, mistress—you will tell me if—"

"Surely. Now go."

Brian tried to open his eyes, but could not. He tried to move, but could not; and realized at length that he was lying on a bed, and that a bandage was on his head and others on his limbs.

Suddenly a hand fell on his cheek, and a thrill shot through him; his beard had been shaved away, for he could feel the softness of the hand against his chin. He felt the hand passed over his mouth—and he kissed it.

There was a startled gasp, then the soft hand returned to his cheek.

"Brian! Are you awake at last?"

"I seem to be," he said, though his voice sounded more like a whisper. "Is that you, Nuala? Where are we?"

"Yes, it is I," came her voice softly, and something warm splashed on his cheek. "Oh, Brian! I so feared that—that you were dead!"

The hand moved away, and he moved uneasily, to feel pain through his body.

"Nay, put back your hand!" he said. He tried to smile. "There, that's better. Where are we, Nuala? On your ship?"

"No, Brian—at Gorumna. But I forgot. Turlough said you must not talk—"

"Oh, curse Turlough," he cried in irritation. "Gorumna? What has happened? Where is the Dark Master?"

"Lie still or I must leave you!" she cried sharply, and he obeyed. "The Dark Master's head is over the gate, Brian. It is two days since the fight."

"Take that bandage from my eyes, Nuala," he said. After a minute her hands went to his head, and as he felt the bandage removed, light dazzled him, and he shut his eyes with a groan. Then he opened them again, and gradually he made out the figure of Nuala leaning over him, while a cresset shed light from above.

"Tell me what has happened," said Brian quietly, as he tried again to move and failed. "Why am I helpless here?"

"Because you are wounded," she replied softly. "Please lie quiet, Brian! I will tell you all that has chanced."

"Where is Cathbarr! Did we win?"

"Yes, we won; but—but Cathbarr—he must have flung away his ax before the ship exploded, for we found it sticking in your boat, and—"

Her voice broke, and a pang of bitterness shot through Brian as he remembered it all now. He groaned.

"And I left him there to die! Oh, coward that I am—coward, and false to my friend—"

A great sob shook his body, but Nuala's hands fell on his face, and there was fear in her voice when she answered him.

"No, Brian—don't say that! If any one's fault, it was Shaun's for not coming sooner to your aid. Cathbarr died as he would have wished, and indeed as he always thought he would die. But now listen, Brian, for I have news."

So, leaning over him, she swiftly told him of what had passed. The O'Donnells had been defeated and slain to the last man; one of their ships was sunk, and the other three captured, and her men held Bertragh. As she and Shaun O'Malley lay refitting and gathering their wounded that same afternoon, a Parliament ship had come in from the south, bearing an answer to the appeal she had sent to Blake at the Cove of Cork.

He had not only sent her powder and supplies, but had sent her a blank commission from Cromwell, which would be filled in upon her definite allegiance to the Commonwealth. The commission guaranteed her possession of Gorumna and Bertragh and the lands she claimed, and promised that when the royalists were driven from Galway the grant would be confirmed by Parliament.

"I am to answer Captain Peyton to-night, Brian," she finished, her eyes dancing. "And Shaun is going to remain and hold Bertragh for me—"

"What's that?" cried Brian. "Hold Bertragh? Am I then wounded so sore that I cannot draw sword again?"

"No," and her laugh rippled out. "Turlough says that you will be as well as ever in a month, Brian. But since you withdrew your fealty to me, I had to find another servant!"

"I had forgotten that," answered Brian moodily. He stared up at her face, and as he met her eyes saw the color flow up to her temples.

"You have slain the Dark Master as you promised, Brian," she said quietly. "And have you forgotten also that you meant to claim a reward from me for that deed?"

Brian laughed, and his face softened as happiness laid hold upon his heart.

"I have not forgotten that, Nuala; but now I am not going to ask that reward in the same way I had intended."

"How do you mean, Brian?" she asked gravely, though her eyes widened a trifle as if in quick fear.

"This, dear lady," he smiled. "When you answer Captain Peyton, let the commission be made out in the name of Nuala O'Neill—and take my fealty for what is left to me of life, Nuala."

He looked up steadily, knowing that all things hung on that instant.

"Well, to tell the truth, Brian," and for a moment she seemed to hesitate, so that Brian felt a sudden shock, "I—I delayed answering him in—in that hope!"

And her face came down to his.

ABOUT THE AUTHOR

H. BEDFORD-JONES is a Canadian by birth, but not by profession, having removed to the United States at the age of one year. For over twenty years he has been more or less profitably engaged in writing and traveling. As he has seldom resided in one place longer than a year or so and is a person of retiring habits, he is somewhat a man of mystery; more than once he has suffered from unscrupulous gentlemen who impersonated him—one of whom murdered a wife and was subsequently shot by the police, luckily after losing his alias.

The real Bedford-Jones is an elderly man, whose gray hair and precise attire give him rather the appearance of a retired foreign diplomat. His hobby is stamp collecting, and his collection of Japan is said to be one of the finest in existence. At present writing he is en route to Morocco, and when this appears in print he will probably be somewhere on the Mojave Desert in company with Erle Stanley Gardner.

Questioned as to the main facts in his life, he declared there was only one main fact, but it was not for publication; that his life had been uneventful except for numerous financial losses, and that his only adventures lay in evading adventurers. In his younger years he was something of an athlete, but the encroachments of age preclude any active pursuits except that of motoring. He is usually to be found poring over his stamps, working at his typewriter, or laboring in his California rose garden, which is one of the sights of Cathedral Cañon, near Palm Springs.

Made in the USA
Las Vegas, NV
24 January 2023

66205131R00125